Every Month Original
Novels, Stories, and Articles

USA Today Bestselling Writer
Dean Wesley Smith

TABLE OF CONTENTS

Short Stories

Full Novel

Serial Novel

Nonfiction

Smith's Monthly Issue #14

Published by WMG Publishing

Introduction
THE FUN AND FREEDOM OF MY OWN MAGAZINE

SOME OF YOU might have noticed that the October issue didn't get to you until the middle or so of November. There really was a good reason for that.

It was the Christmas Issue.

And I tend to hate Christmas before Halloween. Actually, I don't much like it before Thanksgiving, but I couldn't hold the issue that long.

As I described in the introduction last month, I had to write a Christmas novel for a nifty bundle of Christmas books I had been invited into. So I had to push up the Christmas issue of this magazine that I had hoped and planned to do.

I originally planned to have this issue be the Christmas issue, which would have come out in late November.

But honestly, I couldn't make myself ship a Christmas issue before Halloween. Just couldn't make myself do it. Some old traditional bone in my body or something.

So, since this is my own magazine, I decided to hold the October (Christmas) issue until closer to Thanksgiving when a Christmas issue would make sense.

This issue, the November issue, will go out in very early December, the December issue in early January, and then the January issue in late January and the dates on the cover will be back on target.

I know I could have changed the dates or just skipped a month, but I didn't want to do that. So slipping the issues was the best solution.

I know for most of you, none of this will matter in the slightest. It wouldn't for me as a reader. I read magazines when I have time and pay little attention to dates on them. I'm more interested in the stories inside.

But since this is my magazine, and I have the freedom to do what I want without any oversight (which can cause some problems at times, I must admit), I

Thanks for the Support

Dean Wesley Smith

decided to hold the Christmas issue back into the Christmas season, even though it said "October" on the outside.

As for this issue, it's packed with fun stories, including the fourth novel in the Thunder Mountain series, *The Edwards Mansion*. The novel originated from a short story I had in *Fiction River* a year or so ago. It was a Christmas story, but when I looked back at the short story, all I could see was the novel inside the short story that really needed to be told.

So the short story will remain only in *Fiction River*, because I am much happier with the novel here in this issue.

Also starting in this issue is a new serial. A Poker Boy serial story.

Sometime in the spring of 2015, WMG Publishing will rebrand all the Poker Boy stories and novels with new covers that are really, really nifty. But before then, I wanted the readers of this magazine to get a chance to read the short Poker Boy novel that was in *Fiction River* a time back.

The short novel (or novella as some people call them) is called *They're Back: A Poker Boy Short Novel.*

So starting this issue and running for four issues total, I will be serializing the short Poker Boy novel. The short novel is the sequel to the Poker Boy novel *The Slots of Saturn* that was in *Smith's Monthly #7* and now is out as a stand-alone novel in most bookstores.

And for extra fun, in this issue I also have the Poker Boy short story titled "Sighed the Snake."

Add in three more short stories and this is a jam-packed issue of fiction.

I sure hope everyone enjoys the new Thunder Mountain novel. I had fun writing it.

Until next issue, thanks again for all the support.

Dean Wesley Smith
November 7, 2014
Lincoln City, Oregon

Coming Next Issue in Smith's Monthly

A return to the Cold Poker Gang mysteries in a brand new novel

COLD CALL

Dean Wesley Smith

USA Today Bestselling Writer

A Poker Boy Story

Sighed the Snake

Poker Boy saved the world a number of times, but never from an alien.

With the help of his sidekick, Front Desk Girl and Laverne, Lady Luck herself, Poker Boy must do battle with an alien snake across the only battlefield Poker Boy knows: a poker table.

The stakes are higher than in the original Garden of Eden.

To make matters worse, Poker Boy hates snakes.

SIGHED THE SNAKE

A Poker Boy Story

One

"POKER BOY, the aliens are back."

Stan, the God of Poker, said those exact words to me as I sat in his office next to my sidekick and girlfriend, Patty, aka Front Desk Girl.

His office, glass-walled and floating invisible somewhere high above the Las Vegas strip, had felt cool and comfortable when we had entered from a hidden door at the MGM Grand Casino. The view just took your breath away as Las Vegas stretched out below, surrounded by desert and then mountains in the distance. The walls were invisible, so it felt as if Stan had put office furniture on a floating carpet. Only pictures of great poker players on the walls lined out where the room started and the air outside ended.

As we got seated, a United Airlines jet passed silently to our west, just below us, headed for the airport. I could only imagine what the passengers I could see through the window on that jet would have thought if suddenly Stan's office had become visible out their windows, with Patty and me sitting in front of his desk.

Sometimes Stan kept his office dark and dingy, like a back room at an old, downtown casino, straight out of the mob days. That was when he was in a bad mood or things were threatening. When he let it float above the city, as it was now, you knew Stan was feeling pretty darned good about life with the Gambling Gods.

But his casual statement about the aliens returning rocked me, and I studied his smiling face. Even with my black leather superhero jacket and Fedora-like superhero hat on, I didn't have the power to get a read on Stan. No one could get a read on the God of Poker, which was why he had the job. So I reverted to the most logical way to get an answer. I asked him.

"This makes you happy, the aliens being back?"

Patty had sat forward in her seat at the comment from Stan, her long brown hair flowing over her white blouse and dress slacks, her new uniform for work. She had just recently taken a job as customer relations at the MGM Grand Casino and Hotel, and we had been having lunch in the nifty little Greek place just off the downstairs promenade when Stan called us.

When I'm in Vegas, Patty and I not only work cases together, we are an item. Actually, she's my only item whether I'm in Vegas or not, but I haven't figured out a way to tell her that just yet. As Poker Boy, I'm not known for being a ladies' man, or for having just one woman in my life either. I wasn't sure how she would react, but knowing Patty, she probably already knew. She seemed to sense things about me before I did. I figured it was one of her many superpowers. Thank heavens she didn't play poker.

"Actually," Stan said, "not so much happy as satisfied. I won the pool."

"The pool?" Patty asked, glancing at me with those wonderful brown eyes of hers before looking back at Stan.

"We had a pool as to when they would return," Stan said, his smile getting bigger. "I got it to within a month. We started the pool the day after they left."

"They've been gone since the late 1950s," I said. "I'm impressed."

Stan smiled even larger. "Thanks."

"So, why are we here?" Patty asked, shaking her head and sitting back. She worked the hotel side of the gambling industry. And even though she was a superhero working under Laverne, Lady Luck herself, Patty sometimes just didn't understand the nature of a gambler's need to bet on things. The Gambling Gods had bets running all the time for one thing or another. It was what they did. The alien pool was no surprise to me.

"We need you two to make contact with their representative, find out what they are planning, that sort of thing. Right now he's sitting in a 2-4 no-limit game at the MGM Grand."

"Not over at the Bellagio, huh? I wonder why." I would have figured the aliens could afford the higher stakes.

"Not a clue," Stan said.

Now it was making sense to me. I hadn't been a superhero long enough to have met the aliens the last time they visited the planet, but from what I understood, they loved to gamble, which was why the Gambling Gods ended up being their major contact with the planet Earth. The world governments at the time had hated that, but in the end, had to live with it. I doubted anyone in the current world governments had even been briefed that aliens actually existed, let alone the Gambling Gods. The gods, and the superheroes like Patty and me, tended to stay under the radar as much as we could.

"Is the alien any good at poker?" I asked, smiling at Stan.

Stan laughed. "Not a clue. He's new. Go find out."

The wonderful view from Stan's office faded, and Patty and I moved from sitting in front of Stan's desk to walking down the hallway toward the MGM Grand's poker room. Always took a second for the mind to adjust when Stan did that.

TWO

THE POKER ROOM at the MGM Grand had been remodeled a few years back, and now was in the shape of an hourglass. It usually had a good ten games going at any one time, and ran daily tournaments that were pretty popular around town. They catered mostly to tourists, with a few local pros working the room. The big money and high-stakes games had moved over to the Bellagio a number of years back, but the MGM still had a loyal following and they spread a good game and ran a tight room.

"So, what do we do now?" Patty asked, clearly worried about meeting a real-life alien.

"Stop at the counter and stay close until I figure out what the guy wants. I'm going to take us in as much undercover as I can manage."

I had no idea why I was taking those precautions. It just felt right, and as a superhero and a poker player, I had learned a long time ago to trust that feeling.

Patty reached over and squeezed my hand, then let go, which was a good thing. I always found it hard to concentrate when Patty was touching any part of me. Some parts more than others.

As we neared the room, I brought up my Don't-Pay-Attention-To-Me superpower and covered both of us. Someday I was going to have to give that superpower a better name, but describing the effect it had seemed as good as any name for the moment.

I got a rack of five-dollar chips from the front counter and moved toward the 2-4 no-limit table against one drab-colored wall. Four men and two women sat around the table. The two women were clearly together, clearly from some Midwestern state, and pretending to be in over their heads. They didn't even notice me.

The guy in the number four chair was a local pro named Dan, and he managed to see through my cloak and nod as I sat down. Dan stood no more than five feet tall, and usually wore a dress shirt and tan jacket that made him look more like an accountant taking a break from the office than a professional poker player. But I knew he was as sharp and mean as they came and made good money every day at this table. I had no intention of tangling with him.

The other two men were tourists, both with drinks in front of them, and both more interested in the women than in playing poker. That left the guy wearing a snakeskin cowboy hat, sunglasses, and a western shirt, sitting in the seat to the right of the dealer. The weirdest thing about the guy was his tiny nose and almost complete lack of chin. It was as if his face just sort of blended down into his neck and into his black shirt collar.

I sat down in the chair directly across the table from him and slipped the five hundred in chips out of my rack, stacking them neatly as he watched.

He lowered his sunglasses just enough to show me his dark, black eyes, then grinned without showing any teeth. "Poker Boy, I presume."

Dan jerked at the mention of my name, then just stared at me. Clearly, my reputation had gotten ahead of me. I ignored Dan and focused on the alien.

I got nothing, no read, no sense of any emotion at all.

I dug deep and put my best superhero Poker Boy poker-read on him, getting almost nothing but a strange, dark feel. That was getting me nowhere.

"I don't think I have had the pleasure," I said in return.

"Just call me Snake," the alien said, his voice as close to a hiss as I could imagine a human voice sounding.

I hated snakes. I didn't mention that to him. More than likely, he knew. Instead, I just nodded.

I folded the first two cards the dealer fired my way without looking, then watched as Snake glanced at his and folded as well. He had very thin hair sticking out from under his hat that looked combed back over a dark scalp, and he also clearly had a dandruff problem, since flakes kept falling on his black shirt.

"It's been a long time," I said, aiming at him as much of my Make-Them-Relax superpower as I dared use. "At least fifty years."

"Nah, that wasn't my people," Snake said, again grinning under his sunglasses without really opening his mouth. His leather-like skin sort of moved in waves up his neck to his mouth and then back down and I thought for a moment I heard a faint rustling sound. "We haven't been here for a good ten centuries at least."

Oh, crap! Stan wasn't going to be happy with that information. More than likely it meant he hadn't won the pool after all. And he hadn't told me that there was more than one alien race out there.

I felt my stomach tighten into a tiny fist. I hoped like hell Stan and Lady Luck were listening in on this. And I hoped like hell I had managed to keep my best poker face on when Snake told me he was with a different alien race than we were expecting.

"So, what brings you to our little corner of the poker universe?" I asked, forcing myself to stay as calm as possible.

"Why does anyone come to Las Vegas?" Snake asked, glancing at the two women who were ignoring our conversation and flirting with the two men. One of the women had just pulled the last pot and both were laughing about their luck. I had a hunch they were better than just lucky and this flatlander hick routine was just a ruse to take money. And the two guys were going to be more than happy to give it to them.

Dan, the pro, was just shaking his head at their antics and mostly watching me and Snake. I would wager he wasn't real pleased at how his favorite table had shaped up today.

"So," I said, keeping my attention focused on the alien, "you came across vast distances in space to vacation, gamble, drink, and have sex?"

He nodded, glancing at the two cards the dealer had just given him. "That pretty much describes it."

He put a chip on his cards and again sort-of smiled at me, the rustling of his dry skin clearly loud enough to hear this time. It sent shivers down my back. Did I mention that I really, *really* hated snakes? Especially snakes with a bad dandruff problem.

He raised a smooth hundred and Dan folded at once.

"But mostly," Snake said, again pulling down his sunglasses just enough for me to see the pitch black eyes behind them, "I'm here to see if I can beat the best poker player in the game. You up for a little heads-up action, Poker Boy?"

Now, I had to admit that having the alien call me the best player in the game stroked my ego just a little. I knew I was good, but I didn't think of myself as the best by a long ways.

"What did you have in mind?" I asked as I glanced at my cards and flipped the low pair of fours back at the dealer. Any two cards that would cause that kind of raise from Snake had a small pair beat from the start.

"We each start with a million in chips," Snake said. "When one of us has them all, he wins. Blinds level at five hundred, one thousand."

Every sense in my body, and a couple of my superpowers as well, were screaming there was more to this than a simple game for a million bucks.

"So, what would you do with my million, assuming you won it?" Actually, it would be the Gambling Gods' money, not mine. I was fairly rich, but not rich enough to risk a million against some alien.

Snake smiled again without opening his mouth. Again his skin made that dry rustling sound and I tried not to show the shiver that was running up my back. This guy could really be helped by a little lotion.

The dealer flipped me a pair of tens this time around, and I folded them like they were a seven-deuce off. No point in actually playing at this point in the conversation. One of the women giggled and raised and both of the suckers staring at her chest called. Dan and Snake both folded.

I was talking with a member of the alien race that had caused the legend of Adam and Eve.

Snake reached down under the table and pulled up a golden apple, placing it on the rail in front of him. "I assume you don't remember this."

I stared at the apple for a moment. The thing shone in the casino lights, begging for someone to take a bite out of it. My stomach clamped up so tight, I could hardly breathe. I was talking with a member of the alien race that had caused the legend of Adam and Eve. It sure had been a while since they had been here.

A very, very long time, actually.

"Plucked right from the Tree of Knowledge, I bet," I said, keeping my calm exterior as poker-faced as I could, pretending to not really care.

Snake's thin, eyebrows raised above the top edge of his sunglasses. I had surprised him, and for the first time, my poker sense told me this alien had a weakness.

"I am impressed," Snake said. "I was led to understand that your race in general had no long-term memory, that you destroyed your past, or worshipped it for monetary gain."

"For the most part you're right," I said. "But you still haven't told me what the real bet is."

Snake tapped the apple with a long finger. "Contained in the apple is the design and basics for a good dozen major inventions that would forward your race into the stars." He touched the thing again. "Anti-gravity, time control, teleportation. It's all in here."

I didn't mention to him that the Gambling Gods already had all of those things and humanity would discover them in their own sweet time. I wanted to see exactly what he was after in return.

"Nice," I said. "Worth a million I would say."

Snake shook his head, the rustling so loud this time that even one of the guys staring at the women's chest looked around.

"Your money means nothing to me," Snake said.

"I assumed as much," I said, glancing over at where Patty stood near the main desk. Her eyes were wide and now Stan and Laverne were standing beside her. Clearly they were listening.

I gave Snake the old poker stare. "So what do you want in return if you win?"

"Political sanctuary," Snake said. "And twenty of your acres of land with a privacy dome over it so I can build my own climate-controlled garden to live in."

"And if I win?" I asked.

"You get the information in the apple and I will leave the planet and never return."

I glanced at the poker front desk where Patty now stood alone. Clearly Stan and Lady Luck had heard and were off doing what they needed to do.

"Give me fifteen minutes to talk to my boss, and I'll see what I can do," I said, pushing my chair back and standing.

Snake put the apple away and nodded, glancing down at his new cards. "I'll be right here."

I motioned for the dealer to watch my chips and deal me out, pushed my current cards back at the dealer without looking at them, and headed toward Patty.

THREE

WE WERE TEN PACES down the hall away from the poker room when we suddenly found ourselves in Lady Luck's big office. Stan was pacing in front of Laverne's desk, and she was tapping her fingers, staring at a blank screen on the wall beside her desk.

After a moment an alien that looked exactly like the guy sitting in the poker room came on the screen. Only this guy wasn't hiding his snake-like body with four arms and two legs. He was also golden colored, with streaks of red and blue and bright orange along two sides. I had no idea how large he was compared to the guy downstairs, but he seemed much, much larger on the screen.

Who knew that alien life in the universe would develop from snakes as well as monkeys?

"Laverne," the snake said in perfect British English. "It is always a great pleasure."

"The pleasure is all mine, Commander," Laverne said, bowing slightly.

I just stared, more than likely my mouth open. Not often you see Lady Luck herself bowing to anyone.

"I was expecting your call," Commander said. "I assume you have encountered the Lacit fugitive."

"He is sitting in one of our poker rooms as we speak," Laverne said. "He has challenged Poker Boy to a wager: an apple's-worth of knowledge against political sanctuary in a heads-up game of no-limit poker."

Commander shook his head. "They do love that old apple trick. Their entire race seems to never tire of it. They cause more damage to young cultures than any other race."

"I'll take your word for that," Lady Luck said.

Commander frowned and glanced around at something off screen before going on. "We are not scheduled to arrive for another seventeen of your hours. You would do us a great favor by stalling him without giving him political sanctuary. We have been chasing this fugitive for a great deal of your time."

"What will he do if we don't agree to his challenge?" Laverne asked.

"More than likely flee, *after* doing some very permanent damage to your culture. A couple of those apples in the wrong hands would have a very destructive result on your young culture I am afraid."

Laverne glanced around at me. "Can you keep him playing long enough, Poker Boy?"

I glanced at the golden snake on the screen, then at Lady Luck. "I can, with a little help."

"Come in undetected," Laverne said, turning back to Commander. "Your fugitive will be waiting for you at a poker table in Las Vegas."

"Thank you," the big golden snake said, and the screen went dark.

I sure hated snakes.

Lady Luck turned to me. "What kind of help do you need?"

I glanced at Patty, then back at Laverne. "Can you, without Snake noticing, slow down the time in the casino while we play? Make the seventeen hours actually seem more like four or five? I can hold an all-in player for that long, but not a lot longer I'm afraid."

Laverne and Stan both nodded, clearly understanding what I was asking for. Patty just looked puzzled, so to make sure we were all on the same page, I explained to her what I was thinking.

"The Snake has nothing really to lose, so in a no-limit game, he can just shove in all his chips at any given point. Without me facing him in a one-hand showdown, he can just whittle me down slowly as I keep folding. My problem is that I don't dare win or lose. My assignment isn't to beat Snake, it is to play him for a long time, to a draw. Much, much harder thing to do."

"I get it," Patty said, nodding.

"Let's just hope he came to play," Stan said. "I'll set it up in a private room at the MGM. Give me five minutes."

With that Stan vanished.

"Good luck," Laverne said, her face tight and not smiling.

The big office of the head of all the Gambling Gods faded and Patty and I were left standing in the hallway outside of the MGM Grand poker room.

"I really hate it when Lady Luck wishes me good luck," I said, shaking my head.

"Yeah," Patty said. "That's got to worry you. Means she can't really help you much."

"Great," I said, taking a deep breath. I was used to winning, not playing someone to a draw.

"Ready," Stan said, appearing beside us. He indicated a door off to one side of the poker room.

Patty leaned over and kissed me on the cheek, which for a quick second made me forget about how much I hated snakes and remember how much I really liked her. "Luck," she said.

"It will be interesting, if nothing else," I said, smiling at her. I glanced at Stan. "Think you can slow things down a little?"

"We'll see what we can do," Stan said. "But if he starts to notice, we'll back off and you'll be on your own."

"Just keep the snakebite kit handy," I said, then turned and walked toward the table where the alien sat.

FOUR

"PRIVATE ROOM," I said as I got near the alien, indicating the door. "Chips are being set up. You have yourself a bet."

"Perfect," the alien said, smiling again, rustling his dry skin.

I indicated that the pit boss should cash in our real chips and bring them to us, then led the way into the private room.

A poker table filled the center of the meeting room, and an MGM Grand dealer was sitting ready. Two large stacks of chips of varied denominations were stacked in front of the third chair and the seventh chair, facing each other.

I indicated that Snake should pick and he took the three chair while I shut the door behind us.

I sat down and then pointed upward. "We're being recorded and watched by two casino employees to ensure no problems."

"Understandable," he said. Then he smiled again and even from the length of the table I saw dandruff float down onto his narrow shoulders.

As Stan said, luckily, Snake had come to actually play. So, for the first hour, we traded hands back and forth, pretty much ending up level. I would raise and he would fold, he would raise and I would fold. We saw maybe a dozen flops total, with one or the other of us betting and the other folding. Not the kind of match the television folks would be happy with. In fact, on television, the first hour would mostly be edited right out.

I held a slight advantage of less than eighty thousand going into the second hour, not enough to count in this kind of game.

About ten minutes into the second hour, I caught a pair of kings on the button and raised it twenty thousand. Snake smiled and reraised another fifty. I smooth called and we went to the flop.

A third king hit the flop, but there was also an ace and ten, rainbow, meaning all suits.

Snake, with a rustling sound moved another fifty thousand into the pot.

A smallish bet, which might mean he wanted me to call. I didn't like the feel of it.

I sat back and stared at the board, trying my best to get a read on Snake's hand. More than likely he had aces and had me dead. I doubted he would have reraised with Jack/Queen to give him the straight. And if he had ace/king, I had him dead with two pair.

But the key was, I didn't want to win this pot. If I folded now, I would still be slightly ahead, but I had to fold perfectly, showing him I had a read on him, to keep him under control and playing light.

So, like any good poker player, I went into acting mode. I always figured there should be an Academy Award for poker table acting. Those of us who are pros can act with the best of them. It's also why some damn fine actors become good poker players. They already have part of the skill down solid.

"Let me see if I have this right," I said, smiling at Snake and leaning forward. "You reraised me before the flop, not large, but large enough. Now, with the ace on the board, you come out betting, again not huge, but strong enough to make it interesting. Why do I feel like I'm being suckered into this pot?"

He again lowered his sunglasses and I could see his dark eyes under the lip of his cowboy hat. "You trying to get a read on me, Poker Boy?"

I laughed. "Oh, I already have that," I lied. "You're sitting there with a pair of aces in your hand and trying to sucker me in like I'm one of those rank players out there. Maybe next time."

I flipped my pocket kings toward the dealer, face-up so he could see them.

He stared at my kings for a moment as the dealer scooped them up and then the sound of snakeskin rustling filled the room. Oh, oh, I had made him mad. That snakebite kit might not be such a bad idea after all. I had been right about his aces.

He flipped his two cards to the dealer without showing them to me and started stacking the chips from the pot as the rustling slowly faded.

Why couldn't the aliens have been badgers, or gophers, or even alligators? Anything but snakes.

FIVE

FOR THE NEXT HALF HOUR, Snake shed a lot of dandruff and folded almost everything, and I gained chips on him, slowly working it up so that I had a couple hundred thousand extra on him, enough to fold some hands without being in any danger. If I hadn't been playing an alien snake, I would have said that my play had Snake snake-bit.

But I said nothing. I just hoped time outside of this room was moving a lot faster than it was in this room.

Finally, around the beginning of the second hour, Snake seemed to shake himself, a rustling sound that sent dandruff flying everywhere. I had no idea how much dandruff would be covering the table, the chips, everything, if he hadn't been wearing that cowboy hat. I just hoped the snake he made the cowboy hat from hadn't been a relative.

Or another poker player.

Two hands later, he raised and I folded.

For the next fifteen hands straight, he raised and I folded. He clearly had changed strategy and I was looking tight and weak to him with my play now.

"What's wrong, Poker Boy?" Snake asked as I folded yet another hand. "Afraid to play?"

"No cards," I again lied. Poker players lie a lot to other poker players. Actually, I had folded six perfectly playable hands to his raises. I just didn't see any point in mixing it up yet, since I was still a good hundred and fifty thousand ahead of him and was in no hurry at all.

Three more hands he raised and I folded, then with him raising ten thousand, I looked down and saw the worst hand in poker. Seven/deuce off-suit. So I reraised him fifty thousand.

He stared at me from behind those sunglasses, his face ringed with a coat of dandruff white, then finally folded.

I flipped my cards again face up so he could see my bluff. "Got tired of the bad cards. Decided to play a couple."

The rustling filled the room again and the dandruff flew as Snake shuddered and got even angrier. At this point, he had to know he was way outclassed in this game and that I had a complete read on him, even though I didn't really. One of two things would be his reaction. He would settle into slow, steady play, or he would get even more aggressive.

Luckily, after a small dandruff storm, he settled down and stopped raising every hand, and we went back to exchanging blinds with small raises as we had done the first hour.

In that style of play, with me not having any ability to sense him at all, or his hands, he was dangerous in the long run. But it would take a long time for him to wear me down, and that's what I needed to have happen.

Finally, just under four hours into the game, we had a hand that television announcers would love. I had ace/queen and raised thirty thousand.

He flat called and we went to the flop. I put him on a pair, or maybe a weak ace such as ace/nine. At that point I was fairly certain we were going in mostly even.

Flop came out ace and two eights. I had two pair, aces and eights, but I didn't much like that flop.

He bet out forty thousand and this time I called him.

The next card was a third eight, filling me up. But again, I hated that card more than I wanted to admit. We were either going to tie if he also had an ace, or I was beat with my full house against his quads if he had the forth eight.

He checked.

I checked right behind him.

Dandruff flew, telling me he wanted me to bet. It seemed his tell was his bad skin problem. He had the eights.

The last card was a worthless rag, and he bet out another forty grand, just enough to keep me in. I called him, since I would still be up slightly even losing the pot, and he rolled over ace eight.

I rolled over my ace/queen and Snake said "Nice hand," as the dealer shoved him the chips."

"Nice bet," I said.

So after four hours of play, we were still almost even. So far, I had managed to do what I needed to do.

SIX

BY THE END OF HOUR FIVE, I was a hundred grand behind, all from small pots, and Snake's shirt was almost pure white from the dandruff.

By the end of hour six, I was two hundred thousand behind, and Snake had settled into the pattern that I knew from the beginning would wear me down. In a game where winning and losing were an option, I would have ended this hours ago. It had already gone on a lot longer than I had thought possible.

And I thought the same thing by the end of hour seven. I had pressured him into folding a few hands, being clear that he was beaten, but he had gotten me to fold even more, and now my chips were just over six hundred thousand.

"Be nice to my chips," I said, smiling at him. "They are about to come back my way. I can feel the cards turning."

He just grinned and rustled his skin and shed even more dandruff. "We shall see, Poker Boy. We shall see."

My comment had the desired effect and he started raising regularly again, forcing his play, and for a good dozen hands, I folded everything, pretending to get angry at the cards for not turning, even though I was seeing some perfectly good playable hands.

Then, on the button, I looked down at pocket rockets. Two wonderful red aces.

"It's about damn time," I said, and raised a smooth forty thousand. My comment, of course, would tell any decent poker player I really *didn't* have a strong hand. He just called and sat back in his chair.

Not a good sign. He had a monster hand as well.

Flop came ace/queen/jack, rainbow. He bet out forty thousand, the same bet I had made and I flat called him with my three aces. And then I sat back.

"Interesting," Snake said, looking over the top of his sunglasses at me with his dark eyes.

I said nothing and the turn came a ten. If he had ace/king, he had just hit his straight and I was beat.

Before he could reach for his chips I said, "I wouldn't bet much on that straight until you see the river."

His hand froze over his chips, letting me know I had figured his hand perfectly. And by speaking up, I had told him exactly what I had as well. His straight was the best hand, but I had to get any one of one ace, three queens, three jacks, or three tens to win the hand and two kings to tie him with a straight of my own. Twelve outs were a lot of outs.

At that moment, a shimmering went through the air and I had the sense that a bunch of hours suddenly passed. The door to the room opened and two large, gold-colored, snake-like men walked through, followed by Laverne and Stan and Patty.

In a hissing language I had no desire to learn, the two golden-snake men

moved over behind Snake and made him stand, sending dandruff everywhere like a faint snowstorm.

Snake glanced at the cards and then up at me. "Nicely played, Poker Boy. A match I will always remember."

"As will I," I said. But not because of the poker, but I didn't say that.

"Any chance we can see that river card?" Snake asked.

I nodded to the dealer and he flipped the last card over. Another ten.

I rolled over my aces full.

"I guess it wasn't meant to be," Snake said.

A moment later the three aliens vanished.

"Nice job, again, Poker Boy," Laverne said, smiling at me. Then she, too, vanished.

I can't begin to say, as a poker player, how much I liked having Lady Luck smile at me.

Stan smiled as well. "We owe you one for that." Then he was gone.

Patty kissed me, and for a second I forgot all about snakes, poker, and Lady Luck as I enjoyed the feel of Front Desk Girl welcoming me back to the real world.

"Have I ever told you," Patty said as we turned and headed for the door, "how much I hate snakes."

"Oh, after about five hours of playing poker with one, you get used to them."

She laughed. "You up for a wonderful dinner, on me?"

"I think I need a shower first," I said as we walked arm-in-arm down the hallway.

"Oh, I like that idea, too," Patty said, hugging me even closer. "I'll scrub."

"Only if you use a lot of shampoo," I said. "Dandruff shampoo."

~

Now Available
from all your favorite booksellers in trade paper and electronic editions.

Dean Wesley Smith

USA Today
Bestselling Writer

A Jukebox Story

Our Slaying Song Tonight

Sometimes the special jukebox in the Garden Lounge does more than take a person back to a memory. Sometimes it brings a memory to the bar.

And when that memory shows a murder, Stout and the rest must risk their lives to do the right thing.

OUR SLAYING SONG TONIGHT

A Jukebox Story

One

THE GARDEN LOUNGE functioned like a big family room for a lot of people. Comfortable described it. Earth-tone brown carpet, old-fashioned tables and booths, and no windows to let in the troubles of the outside world. The only way in and out for the people who came for friendship and relaxation was the wooden front door.

And, on Christmas Eve, the old Wurlitzer.

The jukebox sat against the wall beside the long oak bar like a king in a place of honor. Four special crystal drinking glasses with names etched on them over the Garden Lounge logo were in a handmade glass case above the old music machine. A large fern hung from the ceiling beside the jukebox, almost seeming to protect it from the stares of the customers.

The jukebox always sat unplugged and dark. The room's music came from a stereo hidden behind the oak bar. The jukebox was decoration only, except for Christmas

Eve. And even on Christmas Eve I was the only one allowed to plug it in. It was just too dangerous any other way. On this particular Christmas Eve there were only four customers to witness the third annual playing of the jukebox.

"Well, Stout?" Carl said. "Is it time?"

I glanced over at Carl. At six-two, two hundred and fifty pounds, Carl had more muscle than two other normal men. And his hands were so huge that his friends figured that women were afraid to get near him. He had never married, never had children. He spent his interest and his energy on a thriving construction business.

The other two there at the moment were David and his wife, Elaine. David was a pilot for a major airline and only allowed himself to drink on Christmas Eve. He had been my best friend before the jukebox had taken him away two years ago and changed his life. Since he came back with his wife, Elaine, we had again become close friends.

Elaine was a beautiful woman in her early forties, with long brown hair that streamed straight down her back and bright green eyes that caused everyone to ask if she wore contacts. She loved David with every part of her soul.

"All right," I said. I guess it's time."

I moved around the end of the bar and unlocked the glass case above the jukebox, then pulled out a glass with David's name on it and another one with Carl's name. I gazed at the other two glasses and the names of Jess and Fred before closing back up the case. Jess and Fred were old friends I missed seeing. I just hoped that when they left the Garden two years ago on Christmas Eve, they found good new homes. Every year I wished they would drop in to say hi. But they didn't know I was here, or remember the Garden and the time they spent here. So far only David and Carl had found their way back.

I moved around behind the bar, washed out the glasses, and filled them with their owner's regular drinks. Bourbon and water for Carl. Rum and eggnog for David. Vodka tonic in a normal glass for Elaine. And then for me I poured myself a mug of warm eggnog without any booze and held the mug up in a toast.

"To friends," I said, "both here and apart."

"I'll drink to that," Carl said and we all raised our glasses and drank.

"Now, I said, putting my mug down on the bar and pulling out a package from beside the cooler, "for the traditional playing of the jukebox this year I have something special."

Everyone laughed. I supposed that playing a time-traveling jukebox would be considered special enough for most. But I had a hunch that I had something even more special.

I unwrapped the package and held up the record.

"So what's so unique about this?" David asked as I handed the record to him and he turned it over to read the title. "It's just *Jingle Bells*." He shrugged and handed the record to Elaine.

"Before I tell you, I need to know if any of you have any strong memories tied to this song." I first glanced at Carl.

He shook his head. "Just feelings of being a kid and having fun. Nothing strong."

"Good. How about you, Elaine?"

"Same thing as Carl. For me this song has sort of always just been there."

I looked at David and he shook his head no.

"You sure?" I asked.

"Nothing that comes to mind," he said. "Which means we aren't going anywhere. Right?"

"That's what I was hoping for," I said. "This song has just always been there for me, too. With no distinct memories attached to it."

"So what makes it so special?" Carl asked, looking at the record and then handing it back across the bar to me.

"Well, with a jukebox that can physically take a person back in time to the memory that the song brings up, wouldn't you think that the *only* record in the jukebox when I found it was special?"

"You're kidding?" Elaine said.

I shook my head. "Not kidding. Remember I told you I found the old jukebox covered in a back hall of the first bar I tried to run. Well, when I went broke and took the old jukebox out just before the bank padlocked the doors on me, this was the only record in it at the time. It was hidden in a small folder inside the back door. The record and the insides of the jukebox were so covered with dust that when I started fixing the thing up, I missed seeing this record and instead put in one of my own. That was how I discovered that the jukebox sent people back to their memories. I ended up sitting staring at Jenny, my old girlfriend.

I held up the old record and looked at it. "I have never played this record."

"Which is why you asked us about our memories with this song. You're going to play it. Right?"

I raised my mug in another toast. "That's right. And tonight, unlike some Christmas Eves in the past, I'd like my best friends to walk out the front door at the end of the night, not through a memory and a jukebox."

Everyone laughed and drank to my toast. Then I went around, opened up the jukebox, and dropped in the record.

"Ready?" I asked as I shut the top and reached to plug in the jukebox.

"Fire away," Carl said.

"You're not really expecting anything, are you?" David asked.

I shrugged. "Not really sure what to expect. I have a feeling there is something special about this record. And combined with that jukebox, your guess is as good as mine. It is curious that this was the only record in there. I assume that the jukebox's previous owner knew what it could do. This may be nothing more than the song that had memories attached to it for him or her."

"And that owner went back, changed the past, and never got to the point where he owned the jukebox in his new future. Right?"

I shrugged. "One theory. Shall I punch it up and see?"

"Why not?" David said.

So I punched E-34, the slot I had put the record in, and stepped away from the jukebox and back around behind the bar.

What did happen was something I never would have guessed.

TWO

AS THE SONG STARTED, two men shimmered into being in front of the jukebox. The jukebox had never brought anyone *to* the Garden before. Only took them away, into their past memories.

One of men was an elderly gentleman wearing an apron and carrying a towel. He had thick silver hair and a worried expression on his face. I knew immediately from the way he was dressed that he was a bartender somewhere in the late fifties or early sixties.

The other man was almost a boy, with red hair, ragged overalls that hung loose on his thin frame, and a red plaid work shirt with stained elbows. With both hands he clutched a large revolver pointed at the old bartender.

We all instantly jumped and Elaine said something about the Holy Mother. Carl started toward the scene.

"No," I said. "I don't think they're really here."

Carl stopped and we all stared.

I was right. Our movements and the sound of our voices didn't alter the scene we were watching in the slightest. It was as if we were watching them through a one-way window.

"Money!" the boy demanded, waving the gun in the direction to the right of the bartender. His voice seemed distant, almost from down a long tunnel. Yet it was clear. "Just reach into that cash box and pull out a handful."

"Nope," the bartender said, wiping his hands on the towel. "You're going to have to take it yourself if you want it. That money is my money and I ain't giving it away to no child with a gun."

"I could shoot you," the kid said, poking the gun forward at the bartender's stomach.

"But you won't," the bartender said. "will you Billy? In fact, if you give me that gun right now I might not even..."

Just then the kid...Billy...seemed to be startled by something behind him that none of us could hear. He turned and as he did the old man reached out and took hold of the gun.

"It's my daddy's gun," Billy said, fighting to pull the gun back away from the bartender. "You can't..."

The explosion seemed almost too loud for one gun.

Too loud for a vision.

Way too loud for the song playing on the jukebox.

The explosion echoed around and around the bar as we watched the bartender grab his stomach and stagger back against the jukebox. His hitting it didn't disturb the record playing Jingle Bells.

Billy just stood there, holding the gun in both hands, staring as the old bartender slid down the jukebox into a sitting position on the floor, his back against the machine. Blood flooded out from the hole in his apron, turning the white cloth dark.

As the record ended, the old bartender took a deep breath and died.

THREE

THE LAST NOTES of Jingle Bells echoed around above the empty booths and tables as the two figures faded from the Garden Lounge.

After the sound of the struggle and the shot, the complete silence of the empty bar seemed the loudest of all.

"Holy shit," Carl said as he sat back down on his stool and took a long drink from his glass.

"I feel like I want to be sick," David said as he too sat down heavily on his stool. Elaine's face was pure white and she just stood there staring at the jukebox as if it might explode at any moment.

I knew how David felt. My stomach was clamped up into a tight knot and my hands were shaking as I tried to get my mug to my lips to get some of the eggnog to my completely dry mouth.

I had no idea what I had expected, but it certainly wasn't a murder.

"You sure know how to throw a Christmas Eve party," Carl said.

David tried to laugh and Elaine just hiccupped and climbed back up on her stool and put her head down on the bar.

"Christmas Eves tend to be that way around here," I said. "Maybe we'll just skip it next year."

"I'll drink to that," Carl said. And did.

David also took a long swallow from his glass and looked across the bar at me, then over at the jukebox. "So now what are we going to do?"

"I know what I'm going to do." I moved quickly around the bar, pulled the plug on the jukebox and then took the record out. It felt odd touching the record, as if I was holding some person's casket. Carefully I put the record back in the bag I had kept it in all these years. I stood the bag on the back bar and went back to my friends who had been watching.

"You think it was the murder that gave the jukebox its powers?" Elaine asked, sitting up and shaking her head slightly as if it might help put away what she had just seen.

I shrugged. "I don't think so, but I really have no idea. There are electronic parts in that thing that are not in any regular jukebox. I have always thought that what that thing could do was just mechanical. Besides that record hasn't been anywhere near that jukebox since I fixed it."

"So maybe," David said, "those two... ghosts, I guess you could call them, are attached to the song. Or more likely, that record." He pointed at the bag. "And obviously the jukebox."

"But why?" Carl asked. "And how? Makes no sense."

"Maybe we should play it again," Elaine said, "even though I don't want to. Maybe we could try to stop the murder."

"I doubt we could," I said. "It looks like it happened a long time ago. I think Carl is right. This makes no sense. But does a jukebox-time-machine make sense either? Yet there it sits. I think the best thing we can do is just let the record and the machine alone until we get more information."

"I'll drink to that," Carl said and raised his glass.

"That's what you said before the floor show started," David said. "Remember?"

Carl shuddered. "I got to stop saying that."

FOUR

IT TOOK ME most of the next year to dig out all the information about what we had seen that night. The murder had occurred in 1959, in a bar called Danny's in a little town in the northern part of the state. The bartender was the owner of the place, Danny Kline, and his murderer was nineteen year-old Billy Webster. Two witnesses had come in just in time to see Billy grab some money from the cash box and run out the back. They found him two days later on a bus headed south, and the trial was quick and without much doubt as to the outcome.

Initially Billy was sentenced to the gas chamber, but after four years on death row, his sentence was commuted to life in prison. It wasn't until I was reading the account in the old newspaper file about his new sentence that I decided what I would do. Maybe Elaine had been right. Maybe we should try to stop it.

Christmas Eve this year was going to be interesting again.

FIVE

FOR A CHANGE, I had strung Christmas lights around the bar to make it feel more festive. And I had even put up a tree in one corner so that now the bar not only smelled of smoke and stale beer, but it had a faint pine scent. I sort of enjoyed that.

"So what's the big surprise you have been hinting at this year?" Carl asked as I opened the glass case above the jukebox and pulled down two of the special glasses. "Because if it's anything like last year, I think I'm going to just head for home."

"I'll go with Carl," Elaine said. "My stomach didn't settle down for a week last year. And I've got a turkey to cook tomorrow that I'd like to taste."

I laughed and moved back to the well to make everyone their drink. "Nothing to worry about, I hope."

"Sounds threatening to me," Carl said.

I just laughed, but I think David could tell by the way he looked at me that I really was worried. Not so much worried about what I had planned working. But more about the final results. What I was going to do might give away the Garden and everything else, including our lives.

I finished making the drinks and raised my mug of eggnog in a toast. "To friends – and doing the right thing."

"I'll drink to that," Carl said, and this year everyone laughed.

I took a drink and set my mug back on the bar. "We have a special guest this Christmas Eve. He's in my office right now waiting for us to finish our toast. You've all seen him before, but none of you have met him." I smiled at their puzzled frowns and went down the bar to my office door.

"Bill, come on out."

Elaine gasped at the name and Carl said, "I'll be a son-of-a-bitch." as the balding, gray-haired Billy Webster opened the office door and walked over to my side. Twenty-eight years in prison had been hard on him. He had obvious scars and he limped slightly off his left leg. He had a beer-gut stomach and deep, sad eyes. In the two years since his parole he had worked as a janitor for the Elk's Lodge. He nodded to everyone as I did introductions.

"Stout," David said, "are you thinking what I think you are thinking?"

I nodded. "Seemed like a good idea to me."

"But if it works," David said, "and the old bartender stays alive and keeps the jukebox, then you may not be here. Did you think about that?"

I just tried to smile.

"And did you think about the chance that we would be gone, and that would mean..." He turned to look at Elaine and she nodded that she understood. It was because of the jukebox three years earlier that David had been able to go back and save her from dying in a car wreck. If the jukebox wasn't in the Garden Lounge for me to send David back, Elaine would be dead.

"But there is a real good chance it won't work out that way," I said. "And Elaine will be as alive as she is now and all of us will be right here, drinking. Besides, if we hold onto the jukebox when the song ends and the world switches, we remember the old timeline. That's how I remembered you two when you didn't come back."

"But you don't know if Elaine will stay for sure, do you?"

My stomach felt cramped and my hands were sweating. "No, I don't."

Billy cleared his throat. "I came here because you said you might be able to help me. I'm just kind of wondering what this is all about."

"It's about taking one hell of a chance," David said.

"It is at that," I said. "But not for you, Bill. The chance is ours. What we need you to do is simple. There was a song playing on a jukebox when you shot old Danny. Remember?"

Bill nodded.

I picked up the sack from the back bar and pulled out the record. "And this was the song. Right?" I held the label and title up for him to see.

Bill again nodded, this time real slowly. There was a shocked look on his face as he stared at the old record. Then he looked up at me. "How did you know? There is no way that anyone could have..."

"Too long a story to explain right now. But if you would just trust me, I think you may have a miracle handed to you this Christmas evening."

"I don't believe much in miracles," he said, still staring at the record.

"Well," I said, glancing over at where David and Elaine sat with worried expressions. "I do. So you are just going to have to trust me."

God, if I said that one more time I wasn't going to believe it either. I just wished I felt as sure of what I was doing as I sounded.

I led Bill down the bar to the jukebox, opened up the lid and put the record in its place. Then I reached around back of the jukebox and plugged it in.

The colored lights flickered on and a slight hum and the smell of burning dust came from behind the jukebox. I reached into my pocket and pulled out a quarter and handed it to Bill. "Your miracle," I said.

He looked at the quarter and then at me. "You're nuts, you know. I knew I shouldn't have come here." He started toward the front door.

"Wait," I said. "Everyone wants a chance to go back and correct their mistakes. Don't you?"

Bill stopped and turned back to face me. "Of course I do. I wished it every day for twenty-eight long years. But I ain't no fool and damned if I will be taken for one. What is done is done. And that is the way it is and should be."

"Sometimes that is the truth and sometimes not." I said. "I'm just offering you a chance to make up your own mind. Nothing more. It is up to you to take it."

"Mr. Stout, I personally think you are as crazy as they come and I met some crazy ones behind the walls." He glanced down at the quarter in his hand. "But I suppose you have got me this far, I might as well finish your damn game and let you all get your laughs."

I only hoped we would be laughing when this was over.

He moved back to the jukebox and dropped the quarter in.

"All you have to do," I said. "is punch E-34 and think about the night you killed Danny. But give us just a second."

I quickly hurried around behind the bar and slipped industrial strength earplugs to everyone sitting there. "Put these on and think of playing golf or snow skiing or something different when the song starts. Otherwise you'll end up back last Christmas Eve."

"No chance," Elaine said and stuffed the earplugs hard into her ears. "But are we going to see that scene again this year?"

I shrugged. "Don't know. With Bill here anything is possible, I suppose." I nodded to Bill. "Go ahead."

He shook his head in disgust and turned to the jukebox. Carefully he punched up E-34 as I did everything I could do to think about the last round of golf I played.

It worked. The only one of us who disappeared out of the bar that Christmas Eve was Bill Webster. As the song started, he blinked twice and then, with a sad frown on his face, he was gone.

And the murder scene did not show up again.

For that I was grateful.

SIX

I MOTIONED for everyone to grab their drink and move over to the jukebox. I could barely hear the song through the plugs so I watched down through the glass until the record was almost over. Then I motioned for everyone to touch the jukebox. I knew without a doubt that Billy would not kill Danny if he had a second chance. But what I didn't know was how Danny being alive would change the history of the jukebox.

If the history of the jukebox did change and I never found it in the back hallway of my first bar, would we be here now, holding onto the jukebox or not?

I didn't really know.

I tried to smile at David beside me, but he was focused on Elaine, as if his pure mental energy would keep her there. I hoped beyond hope that it would.

Carl was standing near the back of the jukebox, with one hand on the chrome and the other on his drink. As the song ended he raised his glass in a toast motion.

The air around the jukebox shimmered.

And Bill appeared.

I thought for a moment I was going to faint.

He looked over at the bar where we had been sitting and then turned around and faced our stunned faces. He had come back. How the hell had he done that?

I pulled the earplugs out as fast as I could, but David had beat me to the question. "What happened?"

Bill smiled and then laughed a low, almost mean laugh. "I shot the son-of-a-bitch again."

"What?" was all I could manage to say as both David and Elaine backed away from him.

Again Bill laughed, only this time I could tell he was thinking back to what had just happened. "You know, Mr. Stout, I just didn't believe you until I found myself standing there with my daddy's big heavy gun in my hand pointed at old Danny."

"But why did you shoot him again?" I asked. "If you knew where it would take you?"

#1... October 2013

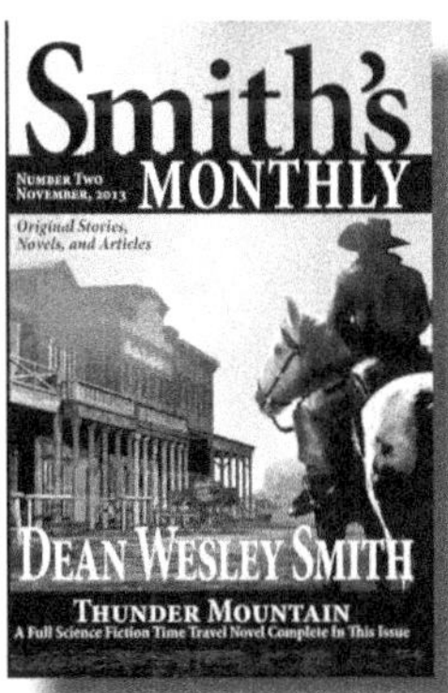

#2... November 2013

#3... December 2013

#4... January 2014

#5... February 2014

#6... March 2014

#7... April 2014

#8... May 2014

#9... June 2014

#10... July 2014

#11... August 2014

#12...September 2014

Bill shrugged. "At first I didn't think I would. But I kept the gun pointed at him and just sort of stood there and listened to that damn song and looked at old Danny and thought. I thought about how I had killed him the first time and about how I had paid my debt. And I thought about the little apartment I have now and my job down at the Elks Club cleaning up."

He faced me directly. "And you know something, I'm a hell of a lot happier now than I was then. My old man was beating me all the time. I was holding Danny up for enough money to get out of town and away from my daddy and his big fists. Well, killing Danny did that for me too. It got me away from that son-of-a-bitch and his fists. He never hit me once after that."

Carl just shook his head and I moved over to a stool and sat down.

"So you shot Danny again?" Elaine asked.

"Yes ma'am," Bill said. "As far as I am concerned, he was dead thirty years ago, so I really wasn't shooting anyone new or alive. But, I did remember what Stout and David here were arguing about. I remember Stout said something about that if I didn't shoot Danny, you might die and he might lose this bar. Now that would be killing somebody new and I just couldn't do that."

Both Elaine and David just stared at Bill with their mouths slightly open.

Bill stepped toward me. "I'd like to thank you for a real nice gift, even though it didn't work out. Not that I pretend to understand exactly how you did it. But as they say on the TV, it is the thought that counts."

He reached out and shook my hand. "Maybe I'll stop by sometime for a drink," he said and then laughed. "But only if you promise me one thing."

I felt more lost than I had in years, so all I could do was nod.

"Promise me you won't play that song while I'm here?"

Finally his words got through the shock I had felt when I saw him reappear. I started to laugh and he joined in and so did Carl and David and Elaine.

"I'll do one better than that," I said after a moment. I stood and leaned over the jukebox and unplugged it, Then I opened the top and took out the old record and with a quick flick of the wrist smashed the record over the edge of the planter beside the jukebox.

"How's that?" I asked.

Bill laughed. "Looks as if you got yourself a new customer."

Both Elaine and David applauded and Carl said, "I'll drink to that."

It took both David and me to stop Elaine from hitting him.

Now Available
from all your favorite booksellers in trade paper and electronic editions.

USA Today Bestselling Writer

DEAN WESLEY SMITH

THEY'RE BACK

A Poker Boy Short Novel

In the first of four parts, Poker Boy and his team must confront the worst enemy they ever faced. The dreaded Slots of Saturn once again.

But the Slots of Saturn died years before. How could they be back?

The sequel to the novel The Slots of Saturn, *this short novel appeared first in* Fiction River.

THEY'RE BACK
A Poker Boy Short Novel

Part 1 of 4

CHAPTER ONE
Not Possible, but Fact

"THE SLOTS OF SATURN ARE BACK," Stan, the God of Poker said to me as he slid into the booth beside Patty.

I laughed and pointed out the window. "Pig just flew by. Pink, a ribbon on its tail. Really flapping hard."

Patty giggled and shook her head.

Stan said nothing, didn't even laugh at my stupid joke.

"Wait, just saw another."

Again he didn't laugh or even shake his head in disgust, which he often did when I got really silly.

Both Patty and I just stared at him, waiting for his punch line. He had just said that the Slots of Saturn were back. That had to be a joke with a really stupid punch line, because those monsters were not a laughing matter.

But no punch line was coming, at least none that I could tell. Trying to get a read on the God of Poker was just about impossible. He had the best poker face on the planet and with his tan slacks, button-down brown cardigan sweater and short brown hair, he could make himself invisible in a crowd without any powers at all.

"Sorry, Poker Boy, Patty," Stan said. "I can't believe it either."

"Serious?" I asked. "No flying pigs with pink ribbons?"

"Serious," he said.

Patty and I had been having a quiet lunch in my invisible office, floating high over the Las Vegas strip. I should have known a wonderful day like today would have a crisis in the middle of it.

Just not this crisis.

Any crisis would be fine except this one.

Patty and I were both dressed in casual jeans and light shirts to spend the day together, since she had a day off from her job at the MGM Grand Hotel front desk. I still had on my black leather coat and fedora-like hat that was my uniform as a superhero. I just didn't feel comfortable going many places without them.

We had plans to tour the Mob Museum that both of us had wanted to see for a year, but hadn't found the time. Then we hoped to have a nice dinner and then go back to her apartment, watch a movie, and see what happened next.

I had been looking forward to that "next" part of the plan all morning.

And lunch in my office had seemed like a great way to start a relaxing and fun day together.

My invisible office floated a thousand feet over the Las Vegas Strip and consisted of four walls of windows and a diner booth smack in the middle of the room. The red vinyl booth had soft seats and could hold eight around the table with room enough for another two to pull up chairs on the end. It was patterned after Madge's imitation 1960's diner my team had met in for years down near Fremont Street in downtown Las Vegas.

An invisible door led from Madge's Diner to this office so that Madge, the waitress (who was also a superhero in the food service part of the gods) could wait on us in here. It was also the entrance for those without teleportation powers.

My office actually served as more of a clubhouse for the members of my team more than anything else. Sitting up here at night on a chair with your feet up on the railing looking out over the city and The Strip was always amazing and relaxing.

After hard days, a lot of the team members did just that.

There was also another invisible door that led to Patty's apartment where we stayed while in town. When we completed our new home we were building in the Oregon Coast Mountains, I would put in a direct door to this office from there as well.

Since Patty didn't teleport, that would allow her to get back to Vegas anytime she wanted from our new home in Oregon.

Patty Ledgerwood, aka Front Desk Girl, was my sidekick and partner and the woman of my heart. We met the first time The Slots of Saturn ghost slots had attacked the city. And we had been a pair ever since.

Now it seemed the ghost slots were back.

Not possible, just not possible.

I just wasn't going to let myself believe it yet.

Madge came through the door from the diner with my cheeseburger and Patty's salad and a big basket of fries. She had already brought us both a large vanilla milkshake to share and had Stan's favorite strawberry shake on her tray as well.

So the ghost slots really were back, even though that was completely impossible.

She slid lunches in front of us and gave Stan his shake. Then she slid the fries over to an open spot at the end of the table and turned to leave without saying a word.

The fries only meant one thing. Laverne, Lady Luck herself, was on the way and had ordered ahead.

So the ghost slots really were back, even though that was completely impossible.

A moment later Screamer, the other original member of our team, and Ben, the oldest and yet newest member of our team appeared and slid into the other side of the booth facing me and Patty.

Screamer had taken part when we rescued over a hundred people from near death in the Slots of Saturn the first time. But wow, that was a long time ago.

Ten years ago, to be exact.

Screamer had the ability, among other things, to get into someone's head and read their thoughts and transfer those thoughts to others. He was a superhero working on the law enforcement side of the gods.

Ben was a god himself, just as Stan was. Ben had been the God of Lamplighters for centuries, but as they didn't need lamplighters as a profession anymore, he had faded. He had spent a lot of time over centuries reading and he remembered every detail. I got him moved over to work with the Gods of Books and Libraries to get him healthy again, and he had became a critical part of our team. He knew history and he knew all the politics and history of the gods. I couldn't believe how much he had helped us so far.

"So what Stan said is true?" I asked, looking at Screamer.

"We got ten people missing so far," Screamer said, nodding, "and my sources with the police think it might be a few more."

"But how?" Patty asked, her voice sounding as stunned as I felt. "We all three stood there outside that warehouse and watched those three slot machines be hauled off to be crushed and destroyed."

I glanced at Stan, who only shrugged. "We don't know, but we've seen security images of the Slots of Saturn appearing and taking someone and vanishing. Just as they did the first time. Exactly, actually. Same spots in the casinos. The locations they appear, that we know about, we now have blocked off."

"So they really are back?" I asked, the fear crushing any idea I had of taking a bite out of my cheeseburger, no matter how good it smelled.

"It seems that way," Stan said. "And we checked and they are not returning to the old Standard Machines warehouse."

"So we don't have any idea where they are stored this time?" I asked. That was how we had managed to deal with them the first time. We found their home.

"No clue at all," Lady Luck said, appearing and pulling a chair up to the table. She didn't grab a fry, but instead just sat there, staring at me.

And when Lady Luck just stares at you, that is not a good sign.

CHAPTER TWO
Searching for a Clue in the Past

GHOST SLOTS had been a myth or urban legend in Las Vegas since slot machines started to become popular. The myth was that a person could pour their entire soul into the machine and thus vanish into the machine.

In other words, slot machines took the souls of people.

I had walked by enough people glassy-eyed in front of slot machines over the decades to think there was some gems of truth in those legends.

And then ten years ago I discovered ghost slots were very, very real when the Slots of Saturn started to attack.

The Slots of Saturn were a three-seat set of very old, very tall slot machines with incredibly-beautiful images of the rings of Saturn all over the machines. You actually had to pull the handle and coins rattled out into the metal tray when you won. They were old machines, retired in the late 1980s and stored in a giant warehouse called a "graveyard."

That's where we had found them through an incredible series of lucky events and teamwork. That day the team had managed to save over a hundred people from the ghost slots.

And we thought we had killed the slots.

Seems we hadn't.

The next two hours we all sat there in the booth, trying to figure out what to do next.

A couple times Lady Luck popped out to check on something, and Stan at one point agreed to talk with the Bookkeeper to see if he could get projections on the machines, assuming no one was controlling them.

Stan said the Bookkeeper was working on it when he came back and would call if he got some results.

The Bookkeeper was a god in the numbers area who never left his house or his computers. He could work a computer and research through the internet faster than anyone in existence. And he had an amazing talent of projecting events that would happen in the future using just numbers.

If someone had learned how to control those deadly slot monsters, then nothing the Bookkeeper could do to project their appearance would help. But if, like the first time, they were just runaway machines hungry for power from those who fed them, aka humans, then they could be predicted.

And the Bookkeeper could do it.

When they took a human, they jumped back to their original location. Then on some hidden schedule that only the Bookkeeper and all his computers could project, the machines would jump again to a location, wait for another victim to sit down and pull the old handle, then with the victim trapped inside the machine, jump back to their original location.

The one limitation ghost slots had was that they could only go back to a place they had occupied in a casino at some point in the past. The problem was that in those days, slots were moved around from casino to casino all the time.

Records of slot movements were hard to find, hard to follow, or had been destroyed by now. There just didn't seem to be much of a reason to save where old slot machines had been thirty or forty or fifty years before and in old buildings now torn down.

Finally, after two hours, Patty and I and Ben were the only three left in the booth. Madge had long since taken away my partially eaten cheeseburger and brought Patty and me another vanilla milkshake.

Lady Luck had jumped off to talk with the gods of law enforcement to see what the real total of missing people might be.

And from exactly where.

Screamer had gone with Stan to talk with the only remaining slot machine tech who had been part of that rescue ten years before. The slot repairman who had triggered the first attack of the Slots of Saturn was now dead.

The three of us were in a wait-and-think mode.

Ben looked like anyone's standard image of the perfect grandfather. Short and square, dressed in a suit without a tie, with short gray hair and a receding hairline. He had a smile that could disarm anyone and now, after a year of working in the area of books and libraries, he had regained his strength from the centuries of being drained in the disappearance of his old job of being the God of Lamplighters.

I sipped on the remains of the milkshake and figured Patty and I needed to order something from Madge pretty soon to keep our strength up. Patty had barely touched her lunch salad as well.

Ben hadn't eaten a thing, even though I offered to buy him something a couple of times.

Patty was sitting beside me, but staring off out the window at a Southwest airliner making an approach into the airport.

"You know," Ben said. "Part of the solution to this might be in how you dealt with these monsters the first time."

"I've been thinking the same thing," I said. "But nothing we did back then seems to matter much this time around. At least not until we find their home and if they are being controlled."

Patty nodded to that.

"So I heard," Ben said, "that you two met fighting these slots. Is that right?"

Patty nodded and smiled, touching my leg, which always calmed me and excited me in a wonderful way, and this touch was no exception.

"We met slightly before we started working on beating the Slots," I said, smiling and putting my hand over Patty's hand on my leg, "but yes, it was the event that pulled us together."

"So tell me about the meeting," Ben said. "I'm becoming sort of the unofficial historian for the gods, and since you two and your team have saved us all a number of times, it seems logical for me to know how all this started."

I honestly didn't know what to say. I wasn't sure how this would help us find the ghost slots, but at this point I trusted Ben and he seemed to think it might be a good use of our time.

Besides, there wasn't one damn thing I could think to do otherwise at the moment.

"You tell your side, first," Poker Boy," Ben said. "Then Patty, you can tell your side of the event."

"The first meeting?" I asked, glancing at Patty. "I honestly can't see how this will help."

"The first meeting," Ben said. "If it doesn't trigger something, then at least it will kill some time here while we wait."

I nodded and sat back. With Patty's hand on my leg, I let myself remember that first meeting with the woman of my life.

CHAPTER THREE
The Memory of that First Meeting

I LOVE CASINOS. Always have.

I mean I truly love them, like some people enjoy sitting beside a calm mountain lake. Walking into a casino, it feels like I've stepped on an ocean beach on a warm evening with no wind, combined with the at-home feel of sitting by a fire, under a nice reading light, with a warm drink and a good book.

I admit, casinos are loud, with both machine and people noises, and are designed by experts to take a person's money. Yet every time I step through the door into a casino, either in Vegas, Atlantic City, or in Timbuck-six North Dakota, I know I am home, that I am safe, that I am in control of my surroundings.

As I stepped through the side door of the Horseshoe that day ten years ago, I walked right into the center of at least forty poker tables. I knew at once I had once again found my own little slice of heaven.

I could feel the power flowing through me. My muscles, tense and tight from the long plane and cab ride, relaxed as if rubbed by a Swedish hot-rub expert.

Now remember, at that point I had only been in the superhero ranks for less than five years, and Stan had pretty much let me go on my own after a little talk or two. So green doesn't begin to describe me when it comes to all this god stuff. I'm still that way.

Ben waved for me to continue, so I did.

I remember that day stopping and just taking a deep breath of the smoke-tainted air of the old casino, filling my lungs with the poisons that killed others, but gave me strength.

Stopping just inside a casino front door was a habit of mine. Still is when I have time.

That day I remember clearly that everything around me looked like a standard day in casino world. And I had no sense that anything was off.

On my right were some of the live poker games, on my left the overflow part of the tournament area, now with all the tables empty. The main desk for the hotel was beyond all the tables, and I had to get there by sort of following the yellow brick road of the pattern on the carpet, through the tables, down between the railings along the live poker tables, and then through the ropes in the open area in front of the hotel desk.

Those ropes that guard the front desks of most hotels and ticket counters in airports always make me feel like a cow being herded to the guy with the hammer who would hit me, put me out of my misery, and turn my body into prime rib and flank steaks. I'm fairly certain some hotels have almost done that to me in the past.

There wasn't anyone waiting in line to check in at that moment. I remember clearly thinking that maybe I could avoid the ropes altogether and just go for the hammer.

I remember putting my head down and moving toward the front desk, pulling my suitcase behind me like a bad child, following the pattern on the carpet, hoping I could get checked in quickly and then take a nap.

I was there for the World Series of Poker which at that point was still held at Binion's Horseshoe Casino. I remember I somehow made it all the way to the front desk without stopping.

"Good afternoon, sir," I remember the woman behind the front desk saying as I stepped up to the polished wood counter.

I remember looking up and honestly, from that point things get a little fuzzy. It was Patty. I remember her smile actually included her brown eyes as she leaned forward a little. And what eyes they are.

"Thank you," Patty said and squeezed my hand.

Ben motioned that I continue and I did.

I think I remember having an out-of-body experience as I studied her eyes.

I knew I could stare into those eyes forever, but I knew I shouldn't.

Yet I remember wanting to.

I remember floating there, arguing with myself, until I finally returned to my body.

"Checking in," I remember that I managed to say, even though my throat was suddenly dry.

"Here for the tournament?" she asked me in return.

I remember saying I was and asking if it was that obvious?

"Poker players do have a look about them," she said to me.

I was in lust with Miss Brown-eyes behind the front desk. I wouldn't learn her name was Patty until later that day.

I gave her one of my many false travel names.

After a moment she said, "Here is your key," and slid the paper packet with the plastic key toward me. I reached for it and her hand brushed mine.

I remember seeing stars!

She wished me, I think, good luck with the tournament, and I thanked her somehow, I think.

Then I turned and tripped over my luggage.

I managed to miss getting tangled in the front desk rope maze as I fell.

That floor may have been carpeted, but I remember it was still hard, and it still hurt.

I remember she leaned over the desk and looked down at me like an angel, the light behind her head giving her a halo, and asked if I was all right.

I thought of staying down, staring at her until she floated over to help me up, then thought better of it.

I sprang to my feet and I somehow managed to not sprint for the elevators.

I looked at Ben and Patty and shrugged. "My side of that first meeting."

Patty squeezed my leg. "You were so cute."

"Falling down was cute?" I asked.

"It was," she said, smiling at me with that same smile I had come to love for ten years.

"So, Patty," Ben said, "tell me your side of what happened."

I looked at her because I realized that in ten years I had never heard her side of that story.

"I knew Poker Boy was coming in for the tournament," Patty said. "And I spotted you at once when you came through the door and stopped. I thought you were cute before you did the dive over the luggage."

"You did?" I asked, stunned.

"Of course," she said, again squeezing my leg. "I had heard a few things about how you had saved some people and a few dogs and stopped Stan from losing his job and all that. So I wanted to meet you."

"Did you know about the Slots of Saturn at that point?" Ben asked Patty.

Patty nodded, which stunned me.

"My boss, Bernice, the God of Hospitality, had been dealing with the missing persons reports all over town. She and I both had a hunch we were dealing with ghost slots, but I honestly didn't want to believe it. None of us did at that point. It was better to think of a more realistic reason than something like ghost slots."

Ben nodded.

I just sat there, surprised.

"So when did you realize you were actually dealing with ghost slots?"

Patty looked at me. "When you and I saw them on the security tape take a customer from the Binion's gaming floor."

I nodded. "That's a memory I'm not going to soon forget."

In fact, just the memory of it right now had me sweating a little.

CHAPTER FOUR
Another Trip to Find a Clue in the Past

BEN ASKED us a few more questions about that second meeting and why we took Samantha, the blind wife of the man who was taken by the slots from Binion's, out of the hotel and to Madge's Diner.

That decision had started our regular meetings for years in the diner and then the design of this office when I built it two years ago.

Going to Madge's had been Patty's idea and my idea to bring in Screamer to help.

Ben walked us all the way through the entire events of that first battle, how we found the slots in the old Standard Slots Graveyard warehouse and how we rescued the people from inside the slots.

Then he asked a very simple question, one that I had a hunch he had been working to for the entire last half hour. "So when was the last time you saw the ghost slots?"

"I remember it clearly," I said. "It was hot, middle of the afternoon."

"A Tuesday," Patty said. "With Screamer, we watched as the two hauling men and two men from Standard Slots hauled the big monster out of the warehouse and craned it up onto a flatbed truck."

"They covered it with tarps and tied it down," I said. "We stood and talked to the Standard men as the two haulers left with it on the back of their truck, headed supposedly to the crusher out at the wrecking yard to the east of town."

Then it dawned on me what I had said. We had a trail, but a ten-year-old trail.

"The truck drivers kept the machine, didn't they?" I said to Ben. "We need to find them and where they kept it the last ten years, or who they sold it to, and we'll have our home for the machines."

I turned to Patty. "You remember the name of the trucking company by any chance? It had a logo on the door."

"Steven's Hauling," Patty said without hesitation.

Damn her memory never ceased to amaze me.

I grabbed my cell phone and dialed The Bookkeeper. Of all the people I knew, he was the best with computers and the internet and research than anyone.

"Still no schedule yet," the Bookkeeper said when he answered the phone.

"Can you trace Steven's Hauling?" I asked. "They picked up the slots ten years ago from the old graveyard warehouse.

"Call you right back," he said.

I hung up and then said, "Stan, we might have a lead."

A moment later Stan appeared with Screamer.

"We're tracking the company that hauled away the slots," I said to him.

"We were trying to find that information out," Stan said, "but the Standard Warehouse Records were long gone. How did you figure it out just sitting here?"

"A short trip down memory lane for Ben," I said, "and Patty's great memory of the name on the truck. Steven's Hauling. I got the Bookkeeper tracing it."

My phone rang.

I answered it and the Bookkeeper said, "Steven's Hauling has been out of business since 2010 when one of their trucks wrecked on the way to LA, killing both of the brothers who owned the company and did all the work of hauling off the slots back ten years ago. Three days after hauling the slots from the warehouse, they deposited three thousand in cash into their bank account that they didn't account for. That was about the going rate for an old set of slots like that back then."

"Nothing else?" I asked.

"All the company records were destroyed in 2012. Now, I'm going back to trying to figure out where these monsters are going to land next."

With that he hung up.

I looked at Patty and Ben and Stan and Screamer. "Dead end. No record of who they sold it to and the brothers who owned and worked the company are dead and all records destroyed."

"And more bad news," Screamer said. "We've got twelve missing so far."

"That the police know about," Stan said.

All I could do was take a deep breath and just wonder what in the world we were going to do to stop this.

Again.

CHAPTER FIVE
Got Them!

PATTY AND I were just about to jump to her apartment, change clothes, and head out for a quiet dinner so we could think when Screamer got a call.

He listened for a moment, then said, "Be right there."

He slipped the phone back into his pocket and said, "Slots of Saturn are in Binion's. Same spot as ten years ago. Police have them surrounded, so no unsuspecting customer is going to jump them at the moment."

Instead of teleporting into a dead camera area, it was just as easy for us to head down through Madge's Diner entrance to my office, out the front door, and across the street to Binion's.

The three slot machines that had haunted my dreams for ten years were there, right where Patty and I had seen them on the security tape all those years ago.

And they looked exactly the same. Exactly.

Bright colors, the images of Saturn and the rings cutting across all three machines, three wooden chairs attached in front of them.

My nightmare had returned in bright, living color.

They were pulsing, dim to bright, every second or so, and I could sense the pull they were putting on people around them, including the police.

Including me.

They were hungry and if they didn't find a victim soon, they might jump.

And when they did, we needed to somehow trace them.

I dropped us all out of time, freezing everything around us. I loved that superpower almost as much as I loved the ability to teleport. All I had actually done was take me and Patty and Ben and Screamer and Stan between instants of time.

But all the casino sounds and the sounds coming from Fremont Street stopped instantly. Also, I could thankfully no longer feel the pull from the slots.

"That thing feels like it's about to jump," I said.

Stan nodded and an instant later Laverne appeared wearing her most distinct black power business suit and her hair pulled back tight. A different look than the last time she had been in my office.

"Got any ideas?" she said, staring at the slots.

"It's about to jump, even if it doesn't get fed," I said. "Do we have anyone who can trace that amount of energy through time and space to figure out where it goes?"

There was a long moment of silence inside an already deadly quiet time bubble.

Then Screamer looked at me, then Stan, and Lady Luck. "Is that machine pouring out a lot of energy?"

"It is," Lady Luck said. "And the energy feels very much human, so like the last time, the thing is being powered by the people inside it."

Screamer then said something that surprised me. "We need Sherri here."

Now Sherri was one of Lady Luck's four daughters and Screamer's wife. They had been separated for some time, a couple of decades from what I understood. But Screamer and Sherri had been working slowly to try to figure out a way to be together. I always knew when he and Sherri had spent time together because he came back smiling.

But at the moment Sherri, who was a superhero, was tending bar in Reno and working for the Gods of Food and Beverage.

She had offered to be part of the team, but until this moment, none of us ever thought to get her involved in any problem.

"Why Sherri?" Lady Luck said a moment before I could.

"She's developed in the last year or so an ability to sense and follow energy," Screamer said. "She can trace a person's energy through a building hours after they walked through it. I think she might be able to trace those monsters, since it's powered by human energy."

Screamer pointed to the frozen ghost slots.

"Didn't know that," Lady Luck said, nodding. "Interesting new type of superpower. Worth a shot. Hold this time bubble and we'll go get her."

Screamer and Lady Luck vanished.

"Did you know Sherri could do that?" I asked both Stan and Patty and Ben.

All of them shook their heads.

"Might be a good power to add into the mix at times," Patty said.

"We shall see," I said, nodding. But I agreed with her. I could think of a couple times that might have been very handy.

An instant later Lady Luck, Screamer, and Sherri appeared.

Sherri was wearing basically the same thing she had on the first time I had met her. Tan slacks, white blouse, and an Eldorado bar apron. She had her long, pitch-black hair pulled back tight, which just accented her stunning beauty.

She and Screamer were holding hands, so I was pretty sure he had transferred to her what was happening. And all the background that had happened ten years ago. He could do that with a touch, let her see inside his head what was happening.

As they appeared, she stepped forward, staring at the Slots of Saturn. "So these are the ghost slots you three defeated ten years ago?"

"They are," Screamer said. "Same damn ones exactly."

"Let's see if I can trace them or not," she said. "Drop the time bubble."

I did as she asked and the sounds of the casino crashed back in around us.

Instantly the wave of energy powered over us from the pulsing slots.

Sherri staggered back into Screamer's arms and collapsed as the slots pulsed faster and faster and faster and then vanished, leaving a newer bunch of slots in its place.

I glanced back at Sherri.

She was out cold and both Screamer and Lady Luck were hovering over her.

A moment later all three of them vanished.

"I'll find out how she's doing," Stan said, and vanished as well, leaving me and Ben and Patty just standing there.

"I think I need a rest," Ben said. "I'll catch up with everyone later."

He vanished.

I looked around at the cops and the people who had been watching all this. And watching all of us just vanish out of thin air. I had no idea how anyone was going to explain all this, or if they would even try, but right at that moment I didn't care.

I jumped Patty and me back to the bedroom of her apartment and stretched out on the bed, not even bothering to take off my leather coat. I used my hat to shade my eyes from what little light was coming around the long drapes pulled closed over the window.

Patty stretched out beside me and took my hand.

"We'll figure it out," she said softly.

I just wished I believed her, because if we didn't, a lot of people were going to die a very ugly death inside a very nasty machine.

To be continued...

USA Today Bestselling Writer

DEAN WESLEY SMITH

I'M HER DEAD HUSBAND

Sometimes ten years with the woman of your dreams might be better than no years. But who wins? You or the woman?

A story of love, dedication, and living a lifetime when faced with reality.

I wrote this story a few years back and never mailed it out, at least to my memory or my scattered records. I really like it, liked it when I wrote it. Not sure why it never got sent anywhere, but now it finds a home here.

I'M HER DEAD HUSBAND

One

TALL GLASS, ice, peach schnapps, orange juice, red straw, and a thin slice of orange.

I finished the Fuzzy Navel and slid it toward the woman across the polished wood bar. "Two-fifty," I said, using my bar towel to wipe water spots off the surface.

I was always wiping up something. This bar might be a smoke-filled dive, but as long as I worked here it was at least going to be a clean, smoke-filled dive.

She dug in her large brown purse, obviously unused to paying for a drink. The older balding guy beside her was making no move for his wallet. He hadn't said a word, but he stood beside her as if they were together.

After bartending for ten years, since my last year in college, I knew, at a glance, which people belonged in a bar and which didn't. But way back on my first night I would have bet anything this lady didn't belong in The Continental Lounge.

And I would have been right.

The older guy she was with was another story. He looked vaguely familiar and a bunch washed out, as if he had spent half his life drinking. I wouldn't have been surprised to see him sliding drunk off of any bar stool in town.

I watched her while she dug for the money. Her dark red hair was conservatively fixed close to her head and pulled back tight. She kept her elbows tucked against her sides, as if opening them up might let everyone know she had tits. She wore a white dress blouse with all but the very top button done up tight. I figured normally she'd have them all buttoned, but tonight she was being daring.

Being in here proved it.

I glanced again at the guy beside her. His face rang bells in my head, but I'd be damned if I could exactly place him. Trying to made my stomach churn.

He was older than her by a good fifteen years and was within a combs length of not having a hair left on his head. He wore what I call the comfortable style: Open necked sweater, no shirt, and soft looking slacks. He looked just plain wrong standing beside the redhead.

Then, while I was looking directly at him, he did the weirdest damn thing. The old dude, just plain as could be, reached down and grabbed her ass.

The woman didn't even flinch and I shook my head.

The things you see in bars never ceased to amaze me. She laid two bucks on the bar mat and went back to searching through her purse for change. Women who looked for exact change in a bar were no-tippers. Guaranteed. Amazing how cheap some people could be.

Of course, with her I doubted if she knew any better. Yet she stood there letting some old guy grab her ass.

Go figure.

I was still waiting and she was still digging when the bald dude reached up and placed his hand on her left tit. He didn't squeeze or nothing. Just held it there.

Again she didn't seem to notice.

"Wait 'til you get outside, would you?" I said to the guy.

He looked up at me and smiled. "So I'm right," he said, taking his hand off her tit. "It's the time."

He looked at me real carefully. "But I almost didn't recognize—"

He stopped as she found two quarters and laid them next to the bills.

"I don't know what you're right about," I said. "But don't do that kind of shit at my bar."

"Excuse me?" she said, looking up at me for the first time.

I noticed she had huge brown eyes. Puppy eyes, too big for her thin face. She didn't strike me to be the type to let some jerk grab a quick feel in public.

"Just talking to your friend there." I nodded in the old guy's direction.

She took a quick glance his way, then looked up at me. Her eyes seemed even bigger, and her face had turned a sick white under the light layer of makeup. "You can see him?"

I glanced over at the guy. He was just looking at me, half smiling.

These two were beyond the college weirdos we got in here on a Friday night.

"Two-fifty," I said, counting the money out loud as I scooped it off the bar and put it in the cash drawer. "Thanks."

I started pretending to work at something in the well. Rule number one when it came to strange customers. Ignore them. After a while they usually went and bothered someone else.

"No," the woman said again, reaching across the bar and touching my shoulder. "Please tell me if you can see him."

"Come off it, lady. Of course I can see him. And don't make believe you couldn't feel his hand on your boob, either."

At that, she got real red and her face went from white to a bright pink that sort of blended right up into her dark red hair.

The guy laughed. "Now you've done it."

The woman whirled and shouted at the empty air about three feet to the guys left, "Keep your hands to yourself and leave me alone!"

She grabbed her drink, stalked over to a table and sat down with such force I thought the chair was going to give way.

Wow. One mad woman.

The older guy was laughing, leaning back with his hands tucked into pants pockets.

"I'm her dead husband," he said as if that would explain everything. "But she was fiery like that when I was alive."

Again he laughed as if he had said something funny. "By the way, my name is Dave."

Full moon. That was it. All the crazies hit the bars on a full moon. Documented fact. This Dave guy proved there must be a full moon out tonight, because he was as crazy as they came. I went back to wiping at the bottles in my well, hoping he'd just move away.

But he didn't. Instead, he moved over closer. "Don't believe me, do you?"

"Sure I do," I said.

Second rule when dealing with a nut

---

case. Agree with them and they smile and go away.

"But you don't," he said. "I can tell. And I seem to remember I didn't either. Which means you didn't. Which..." He waved at the air. "Oh, never mind. Here. Touch my arm and I'll prove it to you."

I glanced up. He had his arm stuck straight out over the bar and was holding it there waiting for me to touch it.

Third rule. Humor them. I reached up to touch his arm just above the jacket sleeve.

My hand went right through.

"Christ," I said, yanking my hand back.

"See. Ghost all the way."

I reached out to touch his shoulder.

He let me.

My hand went right though his chest and I couldn't feel a thing. Nothing. Just like I was sticking my hand out in the air.

I pulled my hand back and glanced at it. Nothing wrong. Hell, now I needed a drink. These idiots were starting to make me see things. Not a good sign.

Especially so early in the night.

"Bet you can't touch my leg, either," the guy said.

"No thanks," I said. Then I purposefully laughed. It probably sounded strained. "Tell me how you did it. You really had me going there."

"It's easy," he said. "First you die. Then you find someone who can see you."

"Cute," I said. "Real cute. You want something to drink?"

"Yes, but no thanks," he said. "I'm afraid I couldn't pick it up if you made it for me."

To prove his point, he reached out and stuck his hand through the fruit tray sitting on the bar. Then, for a final show, he put his hand right through a bottle of lime-juice sitting beside the tray. I could see his sleeve inside the bottle, tinted green.

He pulled his hand out and held it up. "Believe me now?"

I didn't know what to think. Part of me wanted to turn and run for the back room as fast as my little shoes could hit the floor. But another part of me was real curious. The part that kills cats won over the part that wanted to take a coffee break.

"I'm not sure," I said. "What exactly do you want me to believe?"

"That I'm a ghost."

"Then the answer is no," I said. "What else would you like me to believe?"

"How do you explain that you can't touch me?"

I shrugged real obviously. "I don't do explanations. I make drinks. Besides, there are a lot of people in here I can't touch. Your wife, for instance."

I pointed in her general direction. She was staring at me. I waved. She looked flustered and turned back to watch the jukebox and the one lone couple dancing in front of it.

"Hell, go ahead," the guy said. "She's single. I've been dead a year now. She's starting to forget me. Soon she won't even remember that I exist."

Rule number four with crazy customers. If the first three rules don't work, be rude to them. That always does it.

"Is she good in bed?" I asked. "Wouldn't want to go wasting my time with some skirt who won't even get on top. Know what I mean?"

But the old guy didn't flinch. He gazed over at his wife and got this faraway look, like he was remembering the first time he got to first base at the old drive in. Then his eyes sort of misted over and I had a twinge of guilt. But only a twinge.

"She used to be real good," he said,

after a moment. "When she wanted to be. No one better. You'll like that."

"I'll what?" I shook my head. This guy had gone way beyond crazy and he was towing me along as if I were a damn trailer. No more.

"Look, if you don't want a drink, why don't you move along. All right?"

"God, I've forgotten," he said, "just how—"

"Can you really see him?" The wife had gotten up and stormed back over to the bar. "I can't believe he followed me here."

"Lady, I really don't know what you're talking about."

"Tell her I still love her," the old guy said. "But that I'm leaving now."

The red head was staring at me as if she hadn't heard a thing the old man said, waiting for me to say something.

"He said he's leaving now," I told her, playing along with their stupid game.

"Is he gone?" she asked, looking around.

"No," I said, glancing at him.

The old guy shrugged. "I can't leave. I'm sort of tied to her. Got to stay close. But I guess I could go outside."

She looked in the direction I had glanced, then back at me. "Tell him I'm leaving. And tell him thanks for spoiling my evening."

She slammed her drink down on the bar in front of me and headed for the door with short, quick steps.

"Looks like we're leaving," he said. "Next time she'll be alone."

"Sure she—"

Right in the middle of my snappy answer, he faded and disappeared faster than a puff of smoke on a windy day.

"Shit," I said and leaned over the bar to check out the floor where he had been standing. Nothing but stains and cigarette burns in the carpet. That did it.

I grabbed a highball glass and poured myself a good solid double shot of well bourbon. I added two ice cubes and a splash of soda, then headed for the back room. I needed a break. It was going to be one damn long night.

TWO

TWO NIGHTS LATER, during the slow time between the business drunks from happy hour and the regular night drinkers, she dropped back into the bar. The ghost guy had been right. She was alone.

I was cutting lime wedges, getting ready for what promised to be a steady night. She came through the door, paused a moment to let her eyes adjust to the dim light, then came over to the bar and sat down on the end stool.

"Hi," she said, almost too softly for me to hear over the song on the jukebox. "Remember me?"

"Sure do," I said, sliding a bar napkin in front of her. "Figure out your problem with that guy?"

I glanced quickly around the bar. He wasn't anywhere to be seen.

She slowly moved the napkin back and forth in front of her real self-conscious like, as if she almost didn't remember. Finally she said, "I'd rather not talk about him."

"Can't say as I blame you," I said, making my voice sound as cheery as I could. "He was a strange bird, that one. What can I get for you to drink?"

She looked up at me with those huge eyes of hers and smiled a soft thank you smile. "I'll try a Fuzzy Navel. I heard they were good."

I don't know if it was right at that moment that I fell for her, or if it was sometime over the next few hours as she sat at the bar and laughed at my stupid jokes. But I know that it was right at that moment that I started noticing how really pretty she was.

About halfway though the evening I finally got around to asking her name.

"Alice," she said. "Alice Rule? What's yours?"

I didn't want to tell her, on account my name was the same as the strange dude who called himself her dead husband. So instead of Dave, I said David. She didn't even flinch. She said she liked that name. Said it was strong and showed character. Maybe it was at that moment that I fell in love.

Hell, I don't know.

Before she left, I asked her out for lunch the next day and she said yes without even a moment's hesitation. She said she worked as a buyer for a local department store and I could pick her up there.

We had lunch together the next few days and every night she came into the bar to sit and talk. After a while the place started to seem empty without her sitting on that end stool.

After a week, the regulars were really starting to take a liking to her. That convinced me even more that she was really someone special.

I'd served some of those folks for years. I knew and trusted their judgment. When they liked a person, it meant something. They really liked Alice and made her feel welcome and safe.

On my night off, six nights after we met, she took me to her apartment to cook me dinner.

The place was a small, tidy, warm one bedroom, with pictures of parents and one sister on the wall, a white fluff-ball of a cat, and a couch that was so soft, you didn't want to get up.

A single woman's perfect apartment.

Dinner was the best chicken I had ever tasted and later she served a perfectly chilled white wine. I didn't have to come back for breakfast and I didn't get much sleep.

Thinking back now, it was odd that not once during that week did we talk about the guy she yelled at the first night. I don't remember, but I suppose I figured it would come up sooner or later and was happy to have it later.

Hell, I had a few things in my past I didn't much like, including an ex-wife I wasn't real excited about.

It wasn't until two full weeks from the day I first saw her that the strange guy appeared again. She was sitting on her normal stool, talking to Wilber, the retired truck driver who was one of the old time regulars. They were laughing about something and I was staring at her from the other end of the bar, thinking about how young and healthy she was looking, when I noticed out of the corner of my eye a slight movement.

I glanced around and there was the bald guy, Dave, sitting at the bar across from me.

He hadn't come in. I knew that. I had been facing that front door and no one had come through it since Wilber. So just how the hell had he gotten in?

I started to ask him, but he held up his hand and put his finger to his lips for me to be quiet.

"Don't let her know I'm here," he said. "I wanted to see how things were going. Got tired sitting out front all these nights."

"Siting out front?"

Little stabs of jealousy cut at my stomach.

He motioned for me to turn my back so Alice and Wilber wouldn't see me talking. "They can't see me," he said. "But they can see you talking."

"We going to start that shit again?"

But I said it so Alice couldn't see me. I stood with my back to her and pretended to be working on something in the well. She was far enough down the bar she couldn't hear me over the jukebox.

"Let me prove I'm a ghost once and for all," the bald guy said.

He stood up. "I'll show you. Then, when you believe me, maybe we can talk." He walked right through the bar, then through the back bar and disappeared into the mirrors behind the call liquors.

"David?" Alice called out as I stared at the mirrors. "Everything all right?"

"Sure is," I said, scooting quickly along the bar until I was in front of her and Wilber. "Just working on getting ready for the night."

I straightened her drink, then gave her hand a squeeze, proud of the fact that I kept my hand from shaking.

She smiled at me. I felt almost guilty for not telling her what was going on. But at the same time, I wasn't sure exactly what I was seeing. And I didn't want to go losing her, scaring her off by being a nut case.

The bald guy came walking out of the mirrors, back through the bar, and sat down on the end stool.

"Need another drink here?" I asked Alice and Wilber, forcing myself to not stare in the bald guy's direction.

Both said no, so I gave Alice's hand another little squeeze and went back to the ghost. He'd made a believer out of me with the walk through the bar routine.

But what the hell did he want?

"Looks like everything is progressing as I remembered it," he said as I moved back into position by the well with my back to Alice.

"You remembered it?" I asked. "You lost me. In fact, you being here has me damn confused, to say the least. Who the hell are you?"

I had a bunch more questions for him, but figured that would be enough to start.

He laughed. "My name is Dave. I'm Alice's dead husband. I told you that. Although, from how young she's starting to look, I doubt if she will remember me. I've been staying outside lately, away from her."

He glanced down the bar at her. "She lives forever, you know. So do you, so do I, only in a different sort of way than her."

I shook my head and laughed. "Hold on one damn minute. Past you name, I didn't follow a word of that."

It was his turn to laugh. "I doubt if you'd believe much more. I know I wouldn't have. Just enjoy while you can."

"Enjoy what?"

"Alice," he said, softly. "The next ten years."

He gazed in her direction and sighed, then glanced back at me. "I only wanted to remind you I was here. You'll understand when your time comes. Maybe you can break the cycle."

"Wait—"

He was gone again. Not even a cloud of smoke. I glanced over the bar at the empty stool, then grabbed a glass and filled it with ice.

Time for me to have a drink.

A very large drink.

THREE

THAT NIGHT at my place I almost got up the nerve to ask Alice about the bald guy. But it had been a long night, I was tired, and Alice was in a "playful" mood, so the question never got asked.

The next day it just didn't seem as important somehow. Not that I forgot about it. I didn't. It was just never the right moment. And after the ghost didn't show up for a while, there seemed to be little point in asking.

Alice spent a lot of nights sitting on her end barstool and over the next month I found out a lot about her past. But not one word was ever said about being married. In fact, her history filled in solid all the way from high school to the night she came into the bar the first time. There didn't seem to be any time that she could have been married. But why would a ghost lie to me? Made no sense.

Two months after we met, we started talking about getting married. She liked the idea.

I liked the idea.

We'd do it and then she'd help me go back to school, finish the master's degree and get a real job.

Of course, by the time we started making those kind of plans I was head over heels in love and not questioning anything. The truth of the matter was, I wasn't thinking about it. I plain didn't want to.

Six months from the day we first met, we were married in the Methodist church downtown, the big one with the huge colored windows and the ten-step altar. We had to climb all ten of those suckers and I was so nervous, I almost didn't make it. Alice held me up.

Before the service, while I was standing in the front of the church waiting for Alice to come flowing down the center aisle, I thought I saw the bald guy in the balcony above the entrance.

He was wearing the same clothes he had on in the bar. He waved, gave me the thumbs up sign, and then disappeared when the music started.

I didn't understand.

FOUR

TEN YEARS and two days later, I died.

And then I understood.

The doctors told Alice it was a massive coronary arrest.

I was forty-one.

The moment I found myself sitting next to her in the hospital waiting room, listening to the news of my death, wanting to comfort her, hold her, I knew I was the bald guy.

As best I can let me explain what I think happened. If Alice had been the one to have died, I don't think I could have survived. We shared everything. We were more in love the last day then the day we were married.

Not that we didn't have our troubles. Turned out that Alice had one hell of a temper. There was no getting in her way when she was mad. I had a drinking problem that almost split us up three years into things. But she helped me though the drinking and I usually laughed at her temper.

Until I died, I didn't really realize how totally dedicated to me Alice was. Obsessed might be a better term. I figured that the first time around, her total dedication was why I got stuck here, couldn't move on into the next life until her attention was turned to someone else.

And that's why she went back.

Back into the past, her past, my past, dragging me with her until she again found me and married me. Her love held me near her like a dog on a leash.

And all those years I hadn't really noticed.

In fact, I'd enjoyed it.

But it isn't anywhere near as much fun now that I'm dead. And somehow, someway, I have to break the cycle.

After the funeral, she had holed up in our house and wouldn't go or do anything. She didn't eat and was losing weight really fast. I figured she was trying to kill herself so that she could join me. Even though I wanted to break the cycle, I couldn't take the thought of her doing that.

That's when I let her see me for the first time.

Scared her something awful.

I guess those first few times I still didn't have the hang of being a ghost. Making yourself visible is no easy task. You'll discover it takes a lot of real concentration and energy. I suppose I looked sort of watery and not all there.

I couldn't tell.

Like Vampires, mirrors don't work for ghosts.

Maybe it was my reappearing that started her returning to the past. At first, she wouldn't admit that I was even there. If I'd have stopped then, stayed invisible, I might have allowed her to get through her grief and on with her life.

But my showing up, trying to get her to eat kept her in our past. The more I was there, the more she regressed. I could feel the years drifting, coming unstuck.

She didn't like me only being a ghost. She wanted me to touch her, hold her or even talk to her for longer than a few minutes at a time.

She wanted me back, alive, the way I had been the day she met me.

That's you. You're me. Now do you understand why I've been telling you all this? Don't talk to her when she comes back into the bar in two days. I'm not strong enough to break the cycle on this end except by telling you this story.

After years of marriage, you'll understand.

But you can end it. Don't let the next cycle start.

At that moment Alice stood up from the table near the jukebox and stormed back over to the bar. "Can you really see him?" she demanded. "I can't believe he followed me here."

I glanced over at the old balding guy who claimed to be my ghost and who had told me the wildest bar story I had ever heard, then back into her huge brown eyes.

"See who?"

She looked puzzled for a moment, then smiled.

She took a long drink off her glass and set it empty on the bar. "What did you call that drink?"

"Fuzzy Navel," I said, sliding the empty over the bar and into the dish rack.

She walked down the bar and pulled out the end stool. "I think I'll have another. I always heard they were good."

The old guy sighed and then vanished without so much as a pop or a wisp of smoke. I saw him again sitting in the balcony of the church the day Alice and I were married.

And it was a wonderful ten years.

USA Today Bestselling Writer

DEAN WESLEY SMITH

You Do What You Can Do

VARIATIONS OF A SCREAM

Each of us face reality in our own ways. Each of us do what we can do.

Elizabeth Beven, in this biting little story, faces her new reality in the only way she can.

This story fits with many of the nursing home stories I wrote.

VARIATIONS OF A SCREAM

THREE A.M.

ELIZABETH BEVEN, eighty-five, sat at a small manual typewriter and picked at the keys with a paced rhythm like a slow drip from a faucet.

Every night she trickled words onto a page in the form of a letter, folded the page with shaking hands, addressed an envelope, and left both letter and envelope together on the top of her typewriter before returning to bed.

The nurse always mailed the letter the next morning before Elizabeth was dressed.

For the past two years Elizabeth had written a letter every night.

Her routine was always the same.

She awoke at 2:30, after four hours sleep, took fifteen minutes to get from her bed into her wheelchair, to the toilet, and then to the typewriter. Writing a letter made her tired and then she could sleep until morning.

Tonight, the letter was to her daughter, Mary.

Mary lived in the city below the nursing home with her husband Greg and two children, Matt and Martha. Mary said she enjoyed getting the letters from her mother, even though she stopped by the nursing home twice a week.

Elizabeth also wrote to her son, Bill, who lived out in California. But she only wrote him once a week and saved doing his letter for the nights when she felt exceptionally awake. Sometimes, she would even add to his letter during the day, but she never told her daughter.

Tonight, the letter was to Mary.

Mary,

Today, as most days, there is very little news to relay. This morning, Mrs. Robinson—you remember her, two doors north down the hall—fell and broke her hip. She's in the hospital downtown now.

My cold I thought was getting never came on. The nurse gave me something for it yesterday, but I didn't take it because it would have made me too tired to write a letter to Bill last night. You know how I get tired every time they give me a pill.

That's all the news. Mostly nothing happens. We sit here and wait for someone to die and then, when they do, somebody else takes their place.

Oh, by the way, would you please do me a favor and bring—

An intense flash of white light suddenly filled the room, startling Elizabeth and causing her to jerk backwards.

Her wheelchair rolled slightly away from the desk as the room rumbled and shook.

She pulled her robe tightly across her with one hand and held onto her chair with the other.

The long curtains over the sliding glass door danced and jerked like puppets on strings.

She could hear glass breaking down the hall and people shouting and screaming.

The floor of the room shook her right up through the wheels of her chair as she bit her lip and held on.

The lights flickered once, came on bright, then went out, leaving only the faint light coming though her curtains. But even in the dark, she could see the letter to Mary as it rattled and fluttered.

The typewriter vibrated sideways toward the edge of her small desk. She wanted to reach out and save it, but didn't dare let go of her chair.

Finally, with almost an audible sigh, the shaking and rumbling stopped. Her typewriter perched on the edge of her desk, threatening to fall at any moment. She quickly moved forward and pushed it back into place.

Noise from the hall replaced the rumbling.

She turned her chair toward the door. Loud running footsteps went past as she reached the handle and held on to it while backing her chair away. Finally, when the door was open far enough for her chair to pass through, she moved forward into the hall.

The hall was empty to the left. A weak, emergency light cast a faint shadow off the tile floor. She could hear a few of the residents calling out for help, but there was no movement.

To the left was a different story.

Emergency lights flooded the nurse's station like spotlights over a stage. One aide was frantically rummaging through drawers behind the desk.

As Elizabeth watched, the night nurse and another aide came running from the medical supply room, their arms full of packages.

The nurse shouted "Quickly!" and all three of them ran in the direction of the front door.

Elizabeth heard the front door slam.

Again, only the noise of the few residents calling out disturbed the night. The empty, bright light of the nurse's station made her shiver.

She turned her chair back into the familiar surroundings of her room.

She stopped in front of her typewriter and tried to think. Maybe there had been an accident out in the front parking lot and everyone was rushing to help. That would make sense.

She would be able to see that from her patio which overlooked the front lawn, parking lot, and the city in the valley below.

She went to the curtains and pulled them halfway open.

Then she unlatched the lock on the sliding glass door, slid it open, and rolled herself out onto the small patio.

It took a moment to realize what she was seeing.

In the distant valley below, the city was burning. Fire seemed to be everywhere, coloring huge clouds of smoke with orange light.

A few of the houses that lined the street below also burned, the crackling of the flames loud against the hills.

In the distance, Elizabeth could hear a woman screaming. Dozens of people milled in the street, watching, running, shouting.

Elizabeth glanced around at what she could see of the nursing home. It seemed to have survived without much damage. She could see a window broken, but nothing more.

She turned her attention back to the city.

On clear nights, she used to imagine that she could see Mary's house through the trees that shaded the downtown area. On nice evenings she would sit and stare out over the city, imagining what it was like at Mary's house that evening with the two grandchildren playing.

She loved to spend time at Mary's house. But, except for holidays, there never seemed to be much chance. Still, she felt lucky to have raised two such fine children. She had always hoped she would live long enough to see her grandchildren grown.

Now the area around Mary's house was nothing but fire.

The entire city was fire, smoke, and orange light.

Carefully, she wheeled herself to the edge of her patio, folded her hands in her lap and watched the flames.

Later, the chill from the night air forced her into movement.

She took one last look at the street below the nursing home. People still moved. A few gathered around a body on the street.

She watched only a moment, then turned and moved back through the door to her desk.

The orange light from the door gave her just enough light to reread her letter to Mary as she held the paper straight up with shaking hands.

After a short moment, she began to type.

Oh, by the way, would you do me a favor and bring my gray sweater. The nights are starting to get a little chilly and you know how I love to sit on my patio.

That's all for now. Hope to see you soon.

Your loving mother.

She signed the letter, addressed an envelope, and very carefully laid both on the typewriter.

~

Now Available
from all your favorite booksellers in trade paper and electronic editions.

DEAN WESLEY
SMITH
USA TODAY BESTSELLING AUTHOR
The
EDWARDS
MANSION
A THUNDER MOUNTAIN NOVEL

Sherri Edwards only wanted to refurbish an abandoned old mansion that carried her family name. Her goal: To bring the mansion back to original glory.

But the ghost of the original owner kept chasing away all workers. About to give up, two friends suggest she go with them into to the past, to see the mansion, meet the original owner, figure out why he killed himself.

The fourth stand-alone novel in the popular Thunder Mountain series.

THE EDWARDS MANSION

A Thunder Mountain Novel

For Kris

A Historical Note

The Edwards Mansion in Boise was torn down in the late 1960s after sitting in ruins for decades. My father noticed it was being demolished and rescued the Edwards' capstone that had the Edwards' name carved into it. It had been over the front door. He donated the stone to the Idaho Historical Society along with photos of the house in its prime. At times the stone and the pictures appear as part of an exhibit of the early history of Boise.

I am a direct descendant of the Edwards in Boise.

That said, everything in this story, including the characters and the actual location of the Edwards Mansion is completely fictional and based roughly on a short story I wrote a number of years back set in my Thunder Mountain series.

PART ONE
A Problem with a Ghost

CHAPTER ONE

September 19, 2016
Downtown Boise, Idaho

THE BROOKS Garden Restaurant hummed with the noise of a busy lunch hour. Dishes clicking, people laughing, faint background music, and the distant traffic on Grove Avenue in Boise.

But the place had so many plants and tables tucked into nooks and corners that even though it was crowded, to Sherri Edwards it didn't feel that way. The high ceilings and dark wood decor smothered in various plants allowed conversation at a normal voice level instead of having to almost shout as happened at busy times in some restaurants.

But just getting to a table in the back sometimes made her feel like she needed a safari guide and a machete to cut back the overgrown green decorative plants.

She loved the place and looked for any excuse to come here, not only for the wonderful atmosphere, but the chicken and specialty cheese salads couldn't be beat. The entire restaurant always had a rich thick pasta smell, as if a waiter was about to bring her a plate of her favorite spaghetti covered in thick red tomato and garlic sauce.

Who knew a jungle could smell Italian.

Her two best friends, Bonnie Kendal and Dawn Edwards sat with her at the four-person wood table tucked back against the wall under a framed photograph of a rolling field of golden hay and the dark brown remains of a tumbled-down wood barn that had once been dominant over the field. Sherri loved how the golden hay, alive and healthy, contrasted with the dark ruin from the past in the picture.

Dawn was Sherri's distant cousin and one of the most respected historians in the country. She worked part-time as a professor at the university, but spent most of her time researching and writing historical books.

Unlike Sherri, who had long black hair and barely made it past five-four in height, Dawn had long brown hair and was taller at five-eight. She exercised all the time and she and her boyfriend, Madison, never seemed to be apart. Sherri felt lucky to pry Dawn away from him even for a lunch date once a month.

Bonnie was even taller at just under six feet. She also had long brown hair and all three of them were within a year of the same age at just over thirty, but Sherri felt that Bonnie and Dawn just seemed older. And the two of them laughed a lot more than they used to.

Bonnie had been her best friend from grade school on through high school and they had stayed in touch over the years of college and became close again when Bonnie and Duster got married and moved back to Boise.

Now Bonnie and Duster were known as two of the top math brains in the world and were richer than both Dawn and Sherri, which was going some. Both Dawn and Sherri had inherited enough money to never have to work, although both of them still did because they enjoyed what they did.

Sherri figured that after earning four degrees in different forms of restoration engineering and architecture, she had damn well better enjoy what she did. That was a lot of years in school and apprenticeships.

Sherri had focused all her life on historical renovation and had published three books on the subject. She flat loved it with a passion, at least most of the time. At the moment she wasn't finding one restoration project fun at all, and not for the standard construction reasons.

The three of them had spent the first half hour of lunch talking about some historical books they all loved, different things happening at the university, and Dawn's new book project on forgotten mining towns of the Pacific Northwest.

Then, as the waiter found his way through the jungle of plants from the distant kitchen and delivered their lunches, and Sherri was about to dig into her sliced-breast-of-chicken salad, Bonnie asked, "How's the renovation going?"

Sherri forced herself to take a bite of the sweet-tasting chicken with the wonderful honey-mustard dressing while shaking her head. "It's not," she finally said.

"What happened?" Dawn asked, looking surprised. "You love that place and I am so looking forward to you bringing it back up to its original glory."

"So was I," Sherri said.

About six months before she had finally managed to purchase the Edwards Mansion out Warm Springs Avenue, sitting on two oak and cottonwood covered acres on a bluff overlooking the Boise River. The wonderful stone and mahogany mansion had not been lived in for over a hundred years, but for eighty of those years it had been maintained by the former owner's estate. Then it had fallen into ruin and she had been working to buy it ever since.

Even though she and Dawn were of no relation to the original owner, it carried their name and had been one of the most amazing show houses of its time in early Boise history.

For Sherri, restoring that mansion was to be her prize project and she planned on living in the mansion after she was done. But that now looked like it was not to be. And failing at the one project she cared so much about was breaking her heart.

"So what happened?" Bonnie asked.

Sherri glanced at her, then at Dawn. Both her close friends were looking very concerned.

"Did you run out of money buying the place?" Dawn asked. "You know I have more than I can spend and would love to help."

"As would I," Bonnie said.

That actually made Sherri laugh and smile at her close friends. "Thanks," she said, "but I also have more than enough money. It's not that."

"Than what is the problem?" Dawn asked.

"You wouldn't believe me if I told you," Sherri said, shaking her head and taking another bite of her salad, letting the wonderful flavor calm the deep anger she was feeling about the project.

"You would be surprised at what we would believe or not believe," Dawn said, and Bonnie laughed lightly.

"Yes, please, tell us," Bonnie said.

"A ghost is haunting the place," Sherri said, blurting it out. "The original owner supposedly killed himself in the mansion in 1902. I can't get any workers to stay because of the ghost. No one will work in there."

"A ghost?" Bonnie asked, leaning forward.

"You're kidding?" Dawn asked.

"I wish to hell I was," Sherri said, jabbing far too hard at her salad, then finally putting down her fork and taking a drink of her unsweetened iced tea. There was little point in taking her frustration out on a helpless chicken salad.

"The mansion went through three owners," Sherri said, "from the time the estate money ran out, and no one could live in there, which is why it fell into the condition it's in now."

"And you've seen this ghost?" Bonnie asked.

"Nope, just heard it," Sherri said. "And trust me, I don't believe in ghosts and that sound scares hell out of me. I can't blame carpenters and the rest for not wanting to work in there. Sounds like some poor guy is being tortured."

"Wow," Bonnie said, sitting back in her chair, her salad half-eaten.

"I had always heard the place was haunted," Dawn said, shaking her head. "Just never believed it to be true."

"Well everyone I try to get to work there believes it," Sherri said, not hiding the disgust she was feeling. She stared at her lunch, wishing this topic had never come up. Now she would never be able to finish that salad.

"No one will work there, no matter the money you pay them?" Dawn asked.

Sherri shook her head. "A couple contractors I hired even ran from the home leaving their tools behind. Contractors don't leave tools. Those things are sacred, yet they did. And now word has gotten out and no one will even think of going in there. I could kill that guy for killing himself and then haunting his own home."

Then she realized how silly that sounded and laughed, as did Bonnie and Dawn.

"So who was this original Edwards?"

Sherri shrugged. "Not a lot is known about him, including his first name. It is just known he killed himself in the mansion on September, 20th, 1902 after building and living in the place for twenty years. He had no kids or heirs that anyone could find."

"One hundred and fourteen years ago tomorrow," Bonnie said.

"That's right," Sherri said, going back to stabbing at her defenseless salad.

Silence settled over the table as the background sounds of the restaurant filtered into their sheltered table. One woman with a shrill laugh had heard something really funny a few tables away, and someone else was clearing off a table close by, clanking dishes and silverware.

Sherri jabbed her salad one more time for good measure and glanced up at her two friends. "You think I'm nuts, don't you?"

"Not at all," Bonnie said. "I'm just thinking we might be able to do something to help."

"Are you thinking what I'm thinking?" Dawn asked Bonnie.

Bonnie nodded.

"No séance or anything silly like that," Sherri said.

"No," Dawn said, smiling at Sherri. "What we are thinking is far, far crazier than that."

Bonnie laughed and pushed back from the table. "Let me call Duster and see what he thinks."

"Wish Madison was in town," Dawn said. "But he can't get away from that conference. But he would love to join this ghost hunt."

Sherri watched as Bonnie walked toward the front door, her phone to her ear.

"Join what?" Sherri asked. She wasn't sure if she liked the sounds of this conspiracy.

"You busy tomorrow?" Dawn asked, ignoring her question.

Sherri laughed. "About all I do is swear at a ghost, so I'm pretty free. Why?"

"We just need a little field trip is all," Dawn said. "Just trust us, we might be able to solve this ghost problem."

"You can get a ghost out of my house by leaving town?" Sherri asked, convinced her two best friends were crazier than she was for telling them about the ghost.

"In a manner of speaking, yes," Dawn said. "Just trust us."

Sherri stared at her friend and cousin and just shook her head. "I got nothing to lose at this point."

And she didn't. Not a thing. If something didn't change, she was just going to have to tear down the old place and that would break her heart.

She went back to stabbing her salad until it was nothing more than shredded lettuce.

CHAPTER TWO

May 30, 1902
Boise Avenue in Boise, Idaho

CARSON EDWARDS pulled the large beveled-glass and maple wood front door of his mansion closed, listening for the latch to click tightly. He had already saddled Sandy, his brown mare, and brought her around from the stable in the back. She was waiting at the foot of the wide front staircase.

Large columns of mahogany polished to a shine supported the tall wrap-around porch. The porch and wide railings were painted white. The mansion itself was built mostly of polished stone mined from a nearby quarry.

He had spent many a wonderful evening on this porch in the comfortable overstuffed chairs, sipping an iced tea, watching the shadows change as the sunset and the occasional wagon or horse traffic bumped along the rough surface of Warm Springs Avenue.

There was a porch almost as big around the back of the mansion as well that overlooked the river. He loved that porch more than this front area, but not by much.

The day had turned warm, but not too warm for an afternoon ride into town and a night of poker in the great Idanha Hotel poker room. The tall cottonwood trees that lined Warm Springs Avenue in front of his home were casting cooling shade, and a slight breeze blowing off the river below his home helped. Perfect evening.

For twenty years, he had loved every day here, from building the mansion to now. But he had no choice. He now had to get ready to move on. It was just time. When the first cold weather set in at the end of September, he needed to be gone.

He climbed into the saddle and turned Sandy up his long driveway toward the avenue, letting her move at her own comfortable pace. A small wagon with one man driving went past and the man tipped his floppy sun hat and Carson tipped his hat back as well with respect.

He didn't recognize the man. More than likely one of the city workers camping out along the river. Back when he built the mansion, most of his carpenters and stonemasons camped out there as well.

Carson was dressed as he always dressed when going out into public. He had on dark jeans, cowboy books, a silk shirt, and dark vest, covered by a light suit jacket. He usually wore a tan cowboy hat with wide brims to keep the sun off his neck and face and this afternoon was no exception.

He loved playing poker and was looking forward to the night's game. That poker room in the basement of the Idanha Hotel being built two years ago had kept him in Boise for two more years than he had originally planned. So now this would be his last summer here, no matter how much he loved his wonderful home.

He only allowed himself twenty years in Boise. Then his work needed to be done and he needed to move on to Europe and do his research. He doubted he would ever return, but he planned to keep the mansion and have it maintained and cleaned just in case.

He would miss it more than he wanted to admit. But his work needed to be done and he just couldn't afford the time to come back to Boise.

But he still had the summer and he planned on enjoying it.

And enjoying the perfect evening ride into downtown Boise.

CHAPTER THREE

September 20, 2016
North End District of Boise, Idaho

SHERRI HAD NO IDEA where her friends were taking her when they picked her up in front of her condo in the north end of Boise. But wherever it was, six a.m. was too damn early. It was still dark for heaven's sake.

The air under the towering oak trees in her neighborhood was chilled and a little damp. Sherri had no doubt that later in the day it would turn warm again, but now the cool nights in Boise gave warning of the winter that was coming.

She was so tired from getting up this early, she didn't even care about the cold or the fact that she was shivering by the time Bonnie's husband, Duster, pulled up. She had leaned against the trunk of a big oak tree near the road and it was damned lucky she was still awake.

Duster was driving a big Cadillac SUV and Bonnie was sitting in the front seat. Dawn was in the back seat.

Duster got out, smiling, something that no one should be allowed to do this time of the day. He was a handsome man, taller than Bonnie at over six foot, and he always wore dark jeans, a western-style silk shirt, and was seldom seen without his long oilcloth duster and cowboy hat. This morning he was without the coat and hat, but Sherri bet it was in the back of the SUV.

Duster took the small overnight bag Bonnie and Dawn had told Sherri to pack and tossed it in the back and closed the hatch.

"Beautiful morning, isn't it?" Duster asked.

"It's the middle of the night," Sherri said. "I'll let you know when morning gets here."

He laughed as Sherri climbed in next to Dawn, who looked almost as bad as Sherri felt. The inside of the large SUV was at least comforting warm, like crawling under a big quilt.

"Six a.m. is not my idea," Dawn said. She handed Sherri a pillow. "Nap time."

"Who likes it this time of the morning?" Sherri asked.

Bonnie just pointed to Duster and shook her head. She also had a pillow in her lap she clearly was about ready to use. From the looks of this, for Bonnie and Dawn, this was a normal occurrence, this ungodly hour of the morning.

After Duster was back in and they were headed off down the road, Bonnie patted her husband on the arm. "Drive safely. The women need a little more beauty sleep."

Duster only laughed. "I'll wake you all for breakfast."

"And where might that be?" Sherri asked softly.

Dawn just shook her head. "Don't ask, just sleep."

Sherri put her head on the large soft pillow that Dawn had handed her and leaned against the door, looking at the shadows from the streetlights. Before the big Cadillac even got off of Harrison Boulevard five blocks from her condo, she was asleep.

The next thing she realized, Duster was pulling the big SUV into a rough graveled parking area and shutting off the car.

"Time for breakfast," he said, his voice far, far too cheerful.

Cheerful in the morning was a shooting offense in Sherri's book. Luckily she didn't carry a gun.

She sat up and stretched. She felt run over by a herd of cattle and places ached she didn't know could ache. In fact, some of those places she didn't even know she had.

Plus she wasn't sure if she had been drooling or snoring or both. At this point, she felt so bad, she had lost the will to care.

She managed to get out into the morning light. The sun was barely up, the air still had a bite to it, but it smelled of sagebrush and felt dry.

They were in front of a small-town diner with a sign so rusted, the name was gone from the front. The highway they had been on was no more than two lanes wide with a large yellow stripe down the middle.

"Where are we?" she asked as she staggered around to the front of the car where Bonnie and Dawn were both stretching. Both of them had on the same basic thing that Sherri had on—jeans, a cotton shirt with a sports bra under it, and tennis shoes. All of them had their long hair pulled back and tied out of the way.

"Murphy, Idaho," Bonnie said. "Near the Snake River and the Oregon border. We have a horse ranch near here."

With that Bonnie turned and followed Duster into the diner.

"A horse ranch?" Sherri asked Dawn.

"They are an amazing couple," Dawn said.

"So why are we going to a horse ranch?" Sherri asked.

"We're not," Dawn said. "Come on, let's get some breakfast."

Sherri tried to stretch again, but it just hurt too much. What she really wanted was some cold water on her face, so she followed Dawn through the old screen door of the diner.

The door made an awful squeaking sound and banged shut behind her, startling her.

The diner smelled like coffee and bacon, but she couldn't believe she was going to eat in here.

Sherri decided that she would have to remember to not take road trips with Duster again. She loved Bonnie and Duster, but for the first time she didn't understand why Bonnie had married him. Being a morning person was grounds for divorce as far as Sherri was concerned.

Of course, so far she hadn't yet met someone she liked enough to even consider marrying, morning person or not. But she knew for certain that when she did meet a man, he would have to hate mornings.

With a passion.

CHAPTER FOUR

May 30, 1902
Idanha Hotel, Boise, Idaho

CARSON HAD SPENT a little longer than normal on the mile ride into town, just enjoying the wonderful late-spring evening, letting Sandy just sort of mosey along.

He checked Sandy with the stable behind the hotel just as the sun was finally setting over the distant mountains in the east and tipped the man a little extra to give her a good brushing.

Then he headed into the wonderful beauty of the new Idanha Hotel. The stone building was six stories tall and dominated the downtown area with its four corner towers.

Tall ceilings with large polished mahogany columns gave the main lobby a look of expensive vastness. Area carpets of varied colors covered the polished wood floors and were covered in overstuffed armchairs and couches that were as comfortable as they looked.

High windows ran from near the floor almost to the ceiling, framed by dark brown drapes, but not covered.

To the right of the main double mahogany and glass doors was the entrance to the dining area. He had had many a fine meal over the last two years in that dining room. It was one of his favorite in town. And maybe in a couple of hours he would take a break from the poker game and come up for a late dinner.

Directly in front of him as he entered the massive lobby space was the large front desk with over a hundred mailboxes behind it. Two men in suits and vests stood behind the desk helping a couple get checked in, from the looks of the large trunk and four leather suitcases piled to one side against a column.

To the left of the main desk was a grand staircase, painted white with mahogany trim and dark wooden stairs that swept up and to the left. Beside it was a metal cage with an elevator, the first in the entire state.

Carson felt it just flat looked dangerous, but the kids in town loved to ride it and the hotel let them in small groups after school twice a week, supervised, of course.

The staircase to the poker room was behind the grand staircase and Carson headed that way, making his way down the well-lit stairs into the smoke-filled large room at the bottom.

From what he could see, there were at least five games going with six men per table. Since it was still early in the evening, the haze of smoke wasn't that thick yet, but later in the night it would be like a cloud hanging at chest high throughout the room.

There was an open seat on the second table on the right and Carson moved that way. He loved the feel of the room and a number of the regulars nodded hello to him.

As he walked, he took his coat and hat off. He was about to ask if he could join the game when the man sitting to the left of the empty seat glanced up.

Carson froze as the man nodded and looked back at his cards.

Duster Kendal.

Oh, shit!

How was that even possible?

And clearly Duster hadn't recognized him.

So how was that possible?

Carson felt like his heart was going to pound out of his chest.

Bonnie and Duster had gotten him traveling in time for his research and books. They had gone with him the first few times in fact.

That had been just four months ago in 2017 time. Since that day, Carson had lived almost eight hundred years in the past, but the reality was that no way would Duster fail to recognize him.

Carson also had been the only one in the mine when he had hooked up to the crystal and come back here from June 9th, 2017. Duster could not have arrived and jumped into the same timeline in the two minutes and fifteen seconds that were passing in the mine.

Carson stood for a moment watching the hand of cards, trying to catch his breath.

Duster again looked around at Carson, but again clearly didn't show even the slightest hint of knowing Carson at all.

Something very strange was going on here and Carson needed to figure it out before he could ever get his mind on his cards. Especially sitting next to Duster.

Carson nodded to the dealer and turned and headed back to the stairs. It looked like he was going to have an early dinner instead of late one.

He had some thinking to do.

CHAPTER FIVE

September 20, 2016
Above the ghost town of Silver City, Idaho

SHERRI STOOD on the flat top of the old mine tailings about halfway up a steep mountain above the old ghost town of Silver City. A mining shack with no windows, and boards so weathered they were gray streaked with brown, managed to stand to one side of the tailings. The shack looked like it was just about to give up the fight and fall down, and she didn't blame it in the slightest.

Behind the shack, she could see rusted ore car tracks leading back into a boarded up mine face.

The mountain had collapsed in on the old mine, closing it off forever.

The air here was thin and getting warm. It smelled of sagebrush and pine. And it was still far too early in the morning for her tastes.

She didn't want to think about how Duster had managed to bounce the big Cadillac SUV up what was no more than a few ruts to get within a hundred yards of this old mine. That had been the roughest ride she had ever remembered taking.

She planned on walking back down.

Between getting up early, greasy eggs and wonderful bacon, and a rough section of mountain climbing by car, Sherri was not impressed with this idea of a road trip. She had been kind of hoping for something with a spa involved and a long massage from a handsome Swedish guy with strong fingers to ease her tension about the ghost.

So far there was nothing about this trip that was easing any tension.

Sherri had her overnight bag in her hand, even though no one had explained why to her. She certainly didn't plan on spending a night camping on this hill.

She pointed to the old mining shack. "So is the ghost of the mine going to come out and tell me how to get rid of my ghost?"

Duster laughed. "Don't worry. We'll meet your ghost."

"I hope he sounds better than he does with me," Sherri said, shaking her head. She was now convinced her friends had lost it.

"It's clear," Bonnie said to Duster.

He turned to Sherri with a serious expression. "We're showing you this because we trust you. Only fourteen other people know about this. Can we ask that you keep this a secret, what we are about to show you?"

She glanced at Bonnie and Dawn, both of who were looking serious.

Sherri shrugged. "I see no reason I would ever tell anyone about whatever this is, unless you force me to get up this early in the morning again. Then all promises are off."

Everyone laughed and Duster took what looked like an old skeleton key out of his pocket and twisted the head on it.

Silently a huge rock beside the caved-in mine tunnel slid open and then behind it a metal door slid silently aside.

"Wow," Sherri said. "That's nifty."

"You ain't seen nothing yet," Dawn said, taking Sherri by the arm and leading her into the small room behind the rock. When all four of them were in, the door slid closed, plunging them into a moment of darkness before the lights came up and another door slid aside exposing the old mine tunnel.

Thick and clearly old wood timbers supported the rock above, and an oar car track went down the middle of the mine. Regular old low-watt light bulbs hung on a cord along the mine, giving the place a golden feel.

But as she looked closer, she realized the entire place had been supported and done in a way to hide the work.

Duster and Bonnie strode off down the tunnel and deeper into the mine. No way in hell she was going to be killed messing around in an old mine, even one clearly redone. Going into old mines had never been one of her interests and it sure wasn't now.

Not even near her bucket list.

"Don't worry," Dawn said, taking her arm and pulling her forward. "The mine has all been redone to be completely safe. It just looks old in case someone manages to get in here. It's made to discourage them."

"Discourages me," Sherri said, "and I could see it has been redone. So you want to tell me what we are doing in this death trap?"

Sherri's stomach was more cramped up around the greasy breakfast than it had been on the ride up the hill. Not a bit of this made any sense, and if it wasn't two of her closest friends acting as if this was normal, she would be running screaming down the mountainside, of that she had no doubt.

"We're going to show you," Dawn said, "Because you wouldn't believe us if we told you."

"Not real fond of the showing part either," Sherri said, but she let Dawn lead her deeper into the mountain.

Now Available
from all your favorite booksellers
in trade paper and electronic editions.

Suddenly, ahead of them, where the tunnel and the ore car tracks on the ground turned to the right, Duster walked right into the rough stone of the wall and vanished.

A moment later Bonnie did the same thing.

Sherri froze in her tracks, blinking to try to clear her mind from what she had just seen. What the hell was going on here?

"Hologram," Dawn said, pulling her forward. "More security. Just close your eyes and I'll get you through it."

Sherri did as told because at this point she didn't even have enough courage to turn and run. She had gotten used to the howling of the ghost in her mansion, but this was just too damn strange.

Dawn guided her ten more steps forward before saying "Clear."

Sherri looked back. She could see the mine tunnel and ore car tracks leading toward where they had entered. It had been a hologram. Wow, amazing.

Scary, flat scary, but amazing.

Dawn led her forward again as Duster and then Bonnie again disappeared through where the tunnel ahead looked like it ended. The wall looked so real, it was as if Bonnie and Duster were ghosts.

And she had had her fill of ghosts at this point.

"Let me guess," Sherri said. "Another hologram."

"This place has a ton of protections," Dawn said. "You'll understand why pretty soon."

"I would think that just being at the top of that goat path of a road would be protection enough," Sherri said.

"You would think," Dawn said laughing, leading Sherri directly at the wall.

At the last moment Sherri closed her eyes again and put up a hand to make sure if there was something solid there, she would feel it before breaking her nose.

Nothing solid.

She looked back at the tunnel. No sign of the hologram looking back. Or even the projectors that built it.

Very, very top notch effects. She might have to talk to Duster about where he got those and how they worked later. She had some restoration projects a great well-placed hologram would really work for.

If she survived whatever they were going to show her.

Dawn let go of her arm and stepped forward toward where Bonnie and Duster stood at long wooden tables, working to pack saddlebags from the supplies around them.

Shelves and shelves of supplies seemed to fill every inch of the cavern walls around her. It looked more like a warehouse store than a cavern.

Lights illuminated the large cavern with high stone ceilings and shelves on all the walls. Old-style clothing hung from racks and there seemed to be a ton of different supplies from various eras of time stacked on rows of wooden tables.

Dawn motioned Sherri over to one table and started to help her take some of her clothes from her day bag and move it to hidden pockets in an old-looking leather saddle bag.

"What exactly are we doing in this cavern?" Sherri finally asked, the fear twisting at her starting to overwhelm her.

"We're going to go meet your ghost," Duster said. "Before he became a ghost."

Bonnie smiled at Sherri from where she was working about ten feet away at a rack of old-style dresses. "Remember, we know math?"

Sherri nodded.

"Duster and I found a way to travel into the past."

"Yeah, right," Sherri said. She didn't much like the fact that her friend Bonnie suddenly sounded totally crazy.

"They are not lying," Dawn said. "It was how Madison and I met. On the way to Boise, I'll tell you about our first trip back into the past. It was eventful, to say the least."

Both Bonnie and Duster laughed at that, which did not make Sherri feel any better. Three of her closest friends were standing in a mine far under a mountain talking crazy-talk.

Not just crazy. Insane, flat insane, talk.

What had she gotten herself into?

"Just pack what Dawn helps you to pack and in a few minutes you'll understand," Bonnie said. "Trust us for a few more minutes."

"You know how crazy you three sound right now?" Sherri asked. "I thought I had it bad with the damned ghost in my mansion."

All three laughed.

"Trust me," Dawn said. "First time they showed me this place, it was everything I could do to not scream and run."

"Been thinking about it," Sherri said.

Again all three laughed and Dawn hugged her around the shoulders. "Trust me, cousin, for a few more minutes is all."

Sherri slowly nodded. She was already this far underground. What was a few more minutes going to hurt?

She really, really hoped she didn't regret that thought.

CHAPTER SIX

May 30, 1902
Idanha Hotel, Boise, Idaho

THE BIG dining room of the Idanha Hotel had the same floor to ceiling high wooden-cased windows as the lobby. A large stone fireplace filled one corner, dominating that part of the room. In the winter, that fireplace kept this room smelling of a wood smoke and very toasty.

Right now the tops of the windows were open allowing in the fresh evening air. The smell of steak filled the room and made Carson's mouth water. He must have been hungry after all.

Carson asked for a seat off to one side in a corner at a four-person table with a white tablecloth and a single wildflower in a vase in the center of the table. He sat with his back to the room and ordered an iced tea, with real ice, and a rib-eye steak with fried potatoes.

Then he asked the waiter for a paper and pen that he could use to make some notes.

After he got the paper, he started listing possible reasons that Duster Kendal was sitting in that poker room in this timeline. He could not have come through the same connection that Carson had come because he was not in the mine when Carson left.

And besides, if he had done that, Duster would have recognized Carson.

So that was out.

Which meant that Duster came through from another timeline.

And even if it was a Duster from another timeline, he would still know Carson, since the chances are, from what Carson understood about how the time travel to other timelines worked, Carson would also be in the other timelines as well.

Carson put the pen down and folded the notes as his steak dinner arrived.

None of this made sense.

He took a bite of the steak and savored the warm juices of the steak as he chewed it, thinking.

Then suddenly he knew the answer.

"Of course," he said out loud.

Luckily no one was close enough to his table to notice him talking to himself.

That Duster in the poker room was from an earlier future time than Carson.

Carson knew that Duster and Bonnie had spent a couple thousand years in the past in different timelines in the four or five years of future time before they met him. It would be logical that Carson would run into them on one of their earlier trips, when they hadn't yet met him in 2017. Especially since he and Bonnie and Duster all seemed to spend a lot of time in Boise.

Amazing it hadn't happened before now.

He folded the paper and put it in his jacket pocket, then went back to eating the wonderful-tasting rib-eye and the perfectly fried potatoes.

By the time he had finished his meal, he knew what he had to do. If he introduced himself to Duster, he might jeopardize what Bonnie and Duster would do when they asked him to go to the mine the first time.

Carson didn't dare do that.

And he wasn't even sure if he should be around Duster much, in case something slipped that gave him away as another time traveler.

Since, in this timeline, Carson was twenty years older than the college grad that Bonnie and Duster met. Carson knew he hardly looked the same. So just having Duster see him here would never trigger a problem in the future.

When he got done with this trip, it was going to be fun to go talk with Bonnie and Duster and tell them what happened. But right now, Carson figured it was better that he be another face in the past for Duster.

Carson paid for his meal and went back down to the poker room. He found an open seat across the room from Duster.

And the night went easily and he won, finally heading back to his mansion just before midnight.

It was halfway back to the mansion that he wondered just exactly how many time travelers from his future were in that room that he didn't recognize.

CHAPTER SEVEN

September 20, 2016
Inside a mountain above the ghost town of Silver City, Idaho

SHERRI MANAGED to hold her desire to run screaming back up the old mine tunnel and into the light of day until she and Dawn got packed. They put in old-fashioned undergarments that did not look comfortable, plus her modern underwear and her sweat pants and tee-shirt she had brought to sleep in.

Also some modern hygiene products were added in a few secret areas of the saddlebag, plus some first aid and pain meds.

"We'll change into riding clothes when we get back in here," Bonnie said, swinging her saddlebag up to her shoulder and following Duster toward a tunnel in the back of the mine.

"We're going deeper into the mountain?" Sherri asked, her panic almost freezing her to the spot. She had never been claustrophobic or afraid of tunnels or caves, but at the moment she was having trouble breathing.

Dawn swung her saddlebag over her shoulder, then took Sherri's saddlebag in one hand. Then Dawn put her other arm around Sherri's shoulders and pushed her forward to follow Bonnie and Duster.

"You are about to see one of the great wonders of the world, maybe the greatest."

"If I live to get to it," Sherri said, trying to catch her breath.

Sherri stumbled along, even though the dirt floor of the cavern was smooth, as they went into another tunnel and through another wall hologram, then past a huge open door and out into light.

Bright, pinkish-colored light.

The light was coming from beautiful crystals covering the walls of a massive chamber.

It didn't register what she was seeing for a few steps out onto the flat, dirt floor of the huge chamber. Then the size and the beauty hit her like a blow to the gut.

She had been inside of the large football stadiums and this place seemed bigger. And as far as she could see the room went down into the mountain with even more huge caverns of crystals. The other rooms seemed to vanish into an impossible distance.

Her mind would not allow her to really take in what she was seeing.

She blinked and tried to focus on something close to her.

Every inch of every wall was covered in crystals of varied sizes. There were massive crystals that were larger than she was to crystals so tiny she could barely see them. The crystals seemed to be growing in clusters and none of them were the same.

And every crystal seemed to glow with its own power.

She had stopped cold and now she could feel her legs start to give out.

She had never been the fainting type, but honestly, when faced with something like this, fainting seemed to be a damn fine option in her opinion.

Bonnie was on one side of Sherri, Dawn on the other.

Sherri knew they were there, but couldn't grasp anything at the moment past "Wow!"

And the intense desire to just faint to the floor.

"Too much, isn't it?" Dawn said.

Sherri tried to nod, but wasn't sure she succeeded.

"Every crystal in this place is the physical representation of a timeline, just like the one we are living in," Dawn said.

"Every decision anyone makes splits off a new timeline, forms a new crystal," Dawn said. "All the crystals in this room are so close to our timeline, it would be impossible to tell the difference."

"In all these crystals, all these timelines," Bonnie said, "the four of us are here right now. If we had decided to not bring you here, that timeline would be caverns down the line somewhere."

"In other caverns, more than likely hundreds and hundreds of caverns away, are timelines where you decided to not tell us about the ghost," Dawn said.

Sherri slowly let what they were saying sink in.

"There have to be millions of crystals in here," she managed to say, both surprised and happy her voice still worked.

"More into the billions," Dawn said, "in just this massive chamber."

Sherri looked around, letting both Dawn and Bonnie steady her. The only thing that marred the walls of crystals was where the door from the other cavern had been punched through and those displaced crystals were stacked neatly to one side of the door.

The flat dirt floor seemed to just go off into the distance like a massive desert floor, slanting downward slightly.

Sitting near one wall to the right of the door was a long wooden table with a wooden box on it. It seemed tiny and out of place in the vast room.

Two cables long enough to reach the nearby wall were there as well and Duster was adjusting something on the wooden box.

"I'm going to go back to the middle of May of 1902," Duster said, "get us all rooms in the Idanha for August, and horses and supplies and will meet you on August 2nd. That should give us enough time to figure out why this ghost guy of yours kills himself in September."

"We are really going to do this, go back to 1902?" Sherri asked as Dawn and Bonnie led her across the smooth dirt floor the twenty steps to the wooden table.

"You want to see how your home looked in its glory, don't you?" Dawn said.

Sherri nodded, stunned at the idea. Her mind just felt clouded over, foggy, as if she was dreaming, or had too many glasses of wine.

"This is the best way to research that then," Dawn said.

"This is how you do your research?" Sherri asked, looking at Dawn.

"Don't tell anyone my secret," Dawn said, smiling.

Dawn gave Sherri her saddlebag and helped her slip it over her shoulder.

Bonnie moved over to Duster and kissed him. "Behave yourself."

"Don't I always?" Duster asked, smiling.

Bonnie didn't answer, just shook her head.

Sherri stood next to the table with Dawn on her left and Bonnie on her right in front of the wooden box. There seemed to be a timing device on the machine and two terminals to attach the cords on the side. The thing wasn't much bigger than a large breadbox, but didn't look like there was any way to open it.

On the wall near the table Duster attached both cables to a crystal with some sort of expansion band that looked like it could grow or shrink as much as needed and still keep the cables attached. He was wearing thick leather gloves and being very careful.

"Why is he being so cautious?" Sherri managed to ask.

"The crystals contain a vast amount of energy," Bonnie said. "We don't know what would happen if someone touched one with a bare hand, and we don't want to find out."

"Oh," Sherri managed to say and was proud of herself for getting that out.

Duster came back to the machine and attached one of the wires to the machine. He then smiled at all three of them.

Sherri had no idea what was about to happen. She just was glad Dawn was sort of holding her up.

"See you all in a few months," he said, putting his bare hand on the box.

Then he attached the other wire and vanished.

"What?" Sherri asked.

There hadn't even been a sound or a cloud of smoke or anything. He was just there and then he wasn't.

Panic again threatened to send her running.

Dawn's firm grip on her kept her from moving.

Bonnie quickly turned the dial on the machine slightly without touching anything but the dial edge, then said, "On the count of three, put your hand on the box."

"Trust us," Dawn said to Sherri, taking Sherri's hand and moving it toward the box.

Sherri was beyond any fight at this point. She was not believing her eyes at all that Duster had just vanished.

"One, two, three," Bonnie said.

They all put their hands on the box at the exact same moment.

And nothing happened.

Nothing.

Now that was a disappointment.

CHAPTER EIGHT

August 5, 1902
Edwards Mansion, Boise, Idaho

CARSON HAD MANAGED to keep out of Duster's notice for the entire summer. Carson mostly stayed at his mansion, working to get it ready to last for as long as possible.

He was going to leave enough money in an estate account to take care of the home for eighty years, in case he wanted to return at any point in that time. But he knew that he didn't dare just be out of town. He needed to fake his own death and set up some warning systems to scare the unwary away. Nothing fancy, but it would do the trick, he knew.

In 2017, an architectural historian had bought the mansion and was working to return it to its former glory, something that made his heart sing. He had seen her picture in the paper and she seemed to be enjoying what she was doing with his home. He loved this mansion more than he wanted to admit and was glad to see the place surviving into his own time.

And from what he saw, she was doing a great job matching everything about the mansion, even though in 2017 that had to be costing her a fortune.

Each trip back into the past, he built the mansion again, using the same workers, the same design, the same craftsmen, the very same materials.

He never changed a thing from one timeline to another. He never saw a reason to.

That way he could enjoy twenty years here before moving on to do his real research and the reason for his trip into the past.

In four months of time in 2017, since his first trip back with Bonnie and Duster, he had lived just under eight hundred years in the past and rebuilt the mansion thirty-one times.

This trip he planned on spending time in Europe to fill in a few details on some events he had already researched, and then he planned on riding on the maiden voyage of the Titanic. Chances are he would die. He certainly had no plan on taking anyone's spot in a lifeboat.

One of the nice things about knowing you could not die in your original timeline, it allowed for many other chances back here in the past. He had died numbers of times already and although he didn't much care for it, it didn't scare him much any more.

He always just found himself back in the mine touching the machine two minutes and fifteen seconds after he left.

Once he was killed on one of his many expeditions to research the Balkan Wars that led into World War One. He had been killed in World War One three times, once trying to survive until the Christmas Truce. He had wanted to write a chapter about the truce, but after being a part of the Christmas Truce on another trip back, he now planned on making it an entire book.

He had twice witnessed the assassination of Archduke Ferdinand, twice he had been on the Lusitania when it was sunk. He had survived that both times.

He had always been passionate about the time period of 1904 to after World War One in Europe and had done his original thesis on the period far before meeting Bonnie and Duster. He was now working on various books on the subject. He hoped to be one of the world's leading historical experts on the time period by 2019.

The hardest part was not only going back and witnessing the events, but finding the collaborating evidence to what he had seen so that modern 2017 readers would allow and give credibility to his research.

Finding that evidence is what took most of his time.

After he did his research this trip and returned to 2017 and filled in his notes and made progress on the next book, he would return to Boise's past again and build the mansion once again.

Thanks to Bonnie and Duster, he could do that as often as he wanted. He considered himself the luckiest man alive.

CHAPTER NINE

August 2, 1902
Inside a mountain above the mining town of Silver City, Idaho

SHERRI STOOD there for a moment with her hand on the box while Dawn and Bonnie stepped back.

Dawn sort of guided her back away from the box.

"Without getting into any of the math of it, what just happened works this way," Bonnie said. "We attach the two cords to a crystal on the wall. That's the physical representation of another timeline that is so similar to our own timeline as to be almost mathematically the same. Maybe in this new timeline in 1970 someone had a child and in this one the child wasn't conceived."

Sherri nodded. "I understand multiple outcomes of a decision or an event."

"That's what all this represents," Bonnie said, waving her hand around at the huge cavern that vanished into the distance into the ground. "Our math proved that all time has a physical representation in matter in what is basically a central hub. This is a tiny, tiny, tiny fraction of that hub for this area of time and space."

"So where did Duster go?" Sherri asked. "How did he pull that off?"

"He went into the past of the timeline the machine is hooked up to," Bonnie said, pointing to the crystal where the wires were attached. "And we are now in the past of that timeline as well."

"If you detach the wire," Dawn said, "than all four of us will appear back in our timeline exactly two minutes and fifteen seconds after Duster left. No more and no less."

"No matter what we do or how long we stay in this timeline," Bonnie said. "You could stay here and grow old and die and only two minutes and fifteen seconds would pass from your life. And you would be very much alive back in the mine in 2016."

"Why the odd time?" Sherri asked, not at all sure she was believing any of this still.

"That comes from the nature of space and time and matter," Bonnie said.

"Beyond me, then," Sherri said.

Bonnie nodded.

Sherri shook her head, still not really buying any of what they were saying. Granted, they had found the most impressive crystal cavern ever imagined. But all this traveling in time and other timelines she couldn't get her mind around.

Bonnie turned. "Let's go see if that husband of mine has gotten himself in trouble or not."

Bonnie went to the big metal door and opened it.

Sherri remembered they had left it open before.

They went out into the big cavern and the lights came up.

"No Duster," Bonnie said, a slight worry in her voice.

Dawn just shook her head and looked worried as well.

"You were expecting him here now?" Sherri asked.

"He was supposed to get us horses and reservations at the new Idanha Hotel in Boise," Dawn said as Bonnie headed toward a rock wall. There she slid back what was clearly a fake panel that covered an instrument of some sort.

"We're here on time," Bonnie said, sliding the panel closed. "It's seven in the morning on August 2nd, 1902."

"Oh, good, yet another early morning," Sherri said.

Dawn laughed.

"Let's see if he's outside."

"What does she mean?" Sherri asked, again trying her best to keep the panic down to a snippy comment or two.

"Welcome to 1902," Dawn said, smiling.

Bonnie was at a rack of dresses taking one old-fashioned dress off a hanger.

"Come on," Dawn said. "You've got to see this, but we have to dress to the time period in case anyone is looking our way."

"This can't be real," Sherri said. "But damned if I can figure out why you guys are playing this joke on me."

"No joke," Dawn said.

She handed Sherri what looked like a cotton dress that buttoned up the back. "Don't worry about buttoning or if it fits. Just slip it over your clothes and put on this hat."

Dawn handed Sherri a wide-brimmed cotton hat with a yellow ribbon on it, perfect high fashion for 1902. She knew that because she had spent far too many years researching historical homes and styles of various time periods.

Sherri slipped on the dress and then followed Bonnie and Dawn back up the mineshaft toward the entrance.

Inside the entrance, Bonnie looked through some kind of scope and shook her head. "It's clear. No one out there at all."

"That's not good," Dawn said.

"What does it mean?" Sherri asked as the door slipped open and the huge rock slid aside letting in the warm morning air.

"More than likely Duster got himself injured or killed doing something in the last few months," Bonnie said, looking almost disgusted at the idea.

Sherri opened her mouth to say something, then shut it as they stepped out onto the top of the mine tailings and the huge rock slid silently into place behind them.

The mine tailing looked a lot newer, not as worn. The old shack that had been about to fall down was standing proud and still had windows in it. And where Duster had parked the big Cadillac SUV in a stand of trees was now nothing more than bare hillside.

The sun was just coming up over one of the tall nearby mountains, and the sky was still slightly red with morning colors. It had been much later in the morning when they had gone into the mine. And warmer. Right now the air out here had a real bite to it.

None of this was possible. Sherri knew that, but she also knew what she was seeing.

"Take a look at this," Dawn said, moving to the edge of the tailings and pointing down the slope.

Sherri did as instructed, trying to make sense of what she was seeing.

Below her was the town of Silver City, Idaho. Not the ghost town, but the actual town.

"Are we really in 1902?" Sherri asked softly.

"We are," Dawn said.

Behind them the shack door slammed shut.

Dawn and Sherri turned to see Bonnie shaking her head. Clearly there was no sign of Duster as she was expecting.

"Why don't you two stay out here. I'm going to go pull the plug and find out what happened to that husband of mine."

"Get our saddle bags from the table," Dawn said.

Bonnie nodded and quickly scanned the area, then turned the top of an old key and the rock slid back.

Bonnie stepped inside and the rock slid closed. It was as if she had never been here. Creepy.

"So we have a minute or so left in this timeline," Dawn said. "Any questions?"

"This is all real, isn't it?" Sherri asked.

"It is," Dawn said. "Bonnie and Duster are two of the greatest mathematical brains to ever live. And Duster's relatives found this place and Bonnie and Duster have been working to understand time and energy and space since they graduated with more doctorate degrees in math than I want to think about. They have recruited a couple of other great young mathematicians and they allow a bunch of us historians to go back in time when we want for research."

"So what is going to happen when Bonnie disconnects the wire from the machine?"

"We will end up back in the cavern two minutes and fifteen seconds after we left in 2016," Dawn said.

"And Duster will be there as well?" Sherri asked.

"He will be," Dawn said. "No matter what happened to him here in this timeline. That's the reality of the math, Bonnie tells me."

"That's a lot to absorb," Sherri said, shaking her head.

"For now just think about seeing that mansion you own in its 1902 glory," Dawn said.

"That would be nice," Sherri said. "If I don't kill the guy who killed himself."

Dawn laughed.

Suddenly, without any feeling or movement or any sound at all, she was standing between Dawn and Bonnie in the crystal cave, hand on the wooden box on the table. And Duster was there, blinking, clearly surprised.

"So what happened?" Bonnie asked her husband as they all stepped back.

"Must have gotten my fool self killed," Duster said, shaking his head. "Last thing I remember, I was riding along the Snake River, making decent time, headed for the ferry. I had gotten a horse from the ranch down the valley from Silver City.

The morning was starting to get warm and I think my horse was spooked by a snake on the trail. Last thing I remember I was going backwards off the horse."

"Broke your fool neck," Bonnie said, shaking her head. She turned toward the open door into the supply cavern. "Let's go have some lunch before we try this again."

"What, I die and you don't even give me a welcome back kiss?" Duster asked, laughing as he followed her.

"Happens too often," Bonnie said.

Sherri just stood there, watching them go, not having any idea what to think.

She didn't even have a snappy comment to make, that's how shaken she was by this entire thing.

Around her the massive beauty of the crystal cavern just seemed to go on forever.

Finally Dawn said, "Come on. We'll answer the thousand questions I'm sure you have while we eat lunch. I know I was almost too stunned to talk the first time I went back."

"Yeah, feeling that," Sherri said, walking with Dawn toward the door.

She had no doubt she was going to wake up at any moment from this very strange nightmare-like dream.

With luck, the nightmare hadn't caused her to pee the bed, because she just hoped the cavern had a bathroom in it. The two cups of coffee at the diner needed to find a new home and quickly.

CHAPTER TEN

August 5, 1902
Idanha Hotel, Boise, Idaho

CARSON ENJOYED the ride into town just as the sun was cresting over the western mountains. The summer sky was a deep blue, with hints of reds shadowing high clouds. The air was still crisp and dry from the night, giving no hint of the warm day ahead.

He just let Sandy set her own pace and enjoyed the mile ride, watching the swallows swarm and dart along the river. Along the way he tipped his hat to neighbors and passing wagons. Boise in 1902 was a very, very civilized place.

And growing quickly. It was still only a small shadow of what it would be in 2017, but the bones of the larger city were now in place.

He loved the cool mornings and he actually enjoyed the hot days. In fact, he knew that every day until he left on September 20th would be hot. But since Boise was on the edge of the high desert and against mountains, the heat never held through the night.

He always remembered clearly these last two months. He was both anxious to get going with his research, while at the same time he really didn't want to leave his beautiful mansion yet again.

This time was no different. And by this point, his life back in 2017 seemed like a distant memory. He planned, as usual, to spend the last two months going back over his notes for his intended research focus for the trip, to put the very reason for the trip into the past back into focus.

Every time he left, he promised himself that on a future trip into the past he would stay and just grow old and die in his mansion, but he had yet to do that. Instead, he had always faked his death and left early in the morning of the 20th of September.

He hadn't played much poker these last few months, because he wasn't sure if Duster was still in town. But now he needed supplies and just at sunrise, when it was still cool, was the time to go get them.

He gave Sandy to the stable behind the Idanha Hotel and went in for breakfast. When on a supply run, he always treated himself to breakfast and for the last two years of his stay in Boise, it was always in the Idanha dining room. They served the best breakfasts in town for those who could afford them.

He loved the big dining room with the tall windows and stone fireplace. It felt comfortable, yet had a formal atmosphere to it that he had come to enjoy. He had never been rich as a kid or in school, but now, because of Duster's training and his trips into the past, he was far, far richer than he could have ever imagined. And in the past he liked what being a person of means got him.

This morning the hotel had the windows of the dining room slightly open letting in a cool breeze. Not enough to chill, but enough to make sure the room was as cool as it could be for the coming warm day.

Since the dining room had just opened at six, he was one of the first in and was seated at his normal table against the far wall. From there he could see everyone who came in as well as passersby on the wooden sidewalk outside the windows along Main Street.

He had just ordered his normal sliced ham, three eggs, and fried potatoes, taken a sip of his black coffee, and was about to open up the *Idaho Statesman* morning paper that he had picked up from the lobby when a woman about thirty entered the dinning room.

She wore a light-blue summer dress with a slightly plunging neckline and a blue sapphire necklace over smooth, perfect skin. She stood no more than five-four if that and was clearly in great condition. Everything about her shouted she was a woman of means.

She carried a wide-brimmed light-blue hat in her hands and she had long black hair that was held up on the back of her head by an ivory comb. Her white skin seemed flushed, which told of either worry, or a few recent days in the sun.

He had never seen her around town before and found himself having trouble breathing. His heart was beating and suddenly the cool morning didn't seem so cool. He seldom saw a woman of such stunning beauty in the past. At least not in Idaho.

And almost never a woman he was instantly attracted to.

But with this woman, all he wanted to do was go talk with her, get to know her, find out her name and where she was from.

It seemed that in each of his times back into the past, he had met a woman along the way, usually in Europe, but never once in the first twenty years here in Boise. In fact, no woman had ever set foot in his mansion while he owned it.

It wasn't that he didn't like companionship. He just hadn't found anyone that attracted him enough to even approach here in Boise, let alone take back to his home with him.

Until now.

Wow, how was this even possible?

He felt like he had been caught off guard and not prepared and he didn't much like that. He forced himself to take a deep breath and relax.

She had dark eyes and her gaze darted from one side of the room to the other, clearly expecting to see someone and being surprised they were not here.

Her wonderful hands twisted at her hat and she seemed instantly uncomfortable, as if she might panic and flee out of the dining room.

Her cheeks flushed pinkish even more.

Her actions seemed very odd, because a woman of clear means, as she was presenting herself, wouldn't feel uncomfortable in this dining room at all. In fact, just the opposite.

And the more he looked at her wonderful face, the more he felt like he knew her from somewhere.

She stood there for a moment, clearly getting more and more worried as she kept glancing back at the doorway behind her and the staircase across the lobby.

A waiter approached her and said something that Carson couldn't hear and she nodded and said something in return.

The waiter led her to a table directly across the large dining room from Carson and held the chair for her to be seated so that she had her back to the wall and was facing him.

She thanked the waiter and he nodded and turned away.

Carson felt he had seen her before, but he would have remembered if he had met her at any point in all the years he had spent in the past. She had a type of beauty he could never forget.

The exchange with the waiter did not seem to ease her tension. In fact, sitting there alone clearly bothered her even more. She didn't know where to look or what to do with her hands. Her gaze stayed focused on the table and then the hat still in her hands.

He couldn't believe he was so attracted to her. He really needed to stop gawking.

He unfolded his newspaper and watched her over the top of it so at least he didn't seem too obvious. He had no doubt that if he went over to even try to calm her down, she would bolt. And that was the last thing he wanted.

Finally, he watched her take a deep breath and clearly calm down some. She clearly had good self-control, even though this situation really bothered her.

A moment later the waiter brought her a glass of water with real ice in it and she thanked him with a smile that took Carson's breath away again.

Wow, she was the most beautiful woman he had ever seen. And that smile could melt a snowdrift in the middle of the winter.

This wasn't really happening. He couldn't really be falling for a woman at first sight.

He watched her take a sip of the water, then another deep breath.

She was clearly getting her nerves more and more under control.

He put the paper down as, for the first time, she started to actually focus on the people in the restaurant around her. He didn't want to be hiding when she looked at him for the first time.

There were only four occupied tables total. An elderly couple sat against the back wall, and two businessmen sat at a table next to the front window.

She looked at both tables for a moment, then focused her gaze on him.

He kept staring back at her, smiling, as she froze.

Suddenly, she seemed very nervous again and her cheeks turned slightly pink once again.

He nodded to her and then looked down at his newspaper as the waiter brought his breakfast.

When he looked back up, she was smiling and looking very relieved as Bonnie and Duster Kendal came in to join her.

Oh, shit! Luckily he had yet to take a bite of his food, or he would have been coughing and causing a scene.

She was from the future as well.

He put the paper up in front of himself and pretended to read as he tried to eat and think.

This was clearly her first trip. No wonder she looked so scared.

And since Duster had not recognized him, she had also come back here before Carson had, before Bonnie and Duster had invited him to the big crystal cavern. But he was certain he had met all the others that Bonnie and Duster had invited before him at one point or another.

So why hadn't he met this woman? He would have remembered her for sure.

A moment later another woman entered and joined Bonnie and Duster and the mystery woman. This new woman he recognized.

Dawn Edwards.

No relation at all to him, but she and her boyfriend Madison had been the first two Bonnie and Duster had invited to the crystal cavern. Both of them were famous historians and he had met Dawn numbers of times over the last few months of his life in 2017.

So before Bonnie and Duster had invited him to use the crystal cavern for his research of Europe and World War One, they had brought this mystery woman back with them. And he hadn't heard about it for some reason.

Then suddenly, he remembered where he knew the mystery woman. He had seen her picture in the newspaper in 2017.

Her name was Sherri Edwards.

She was the historical architect that had bought his mansion and was refurbishing it.

Oh, shit, oh shit, oh shit. They were here to see his home and meet him.

Now what was he going to do?

CHAPTER ELEVEN

August 5, 1902
Idanha Hotel, Boise, Idaho

AFTER AN HOUR having lunch in a kitchen area tucked back in an alcove in the big cavern, Sherri had been in, she was feeling slightly better. The kitchen and the two bathrooms to one side of it were as modern as any kitchen or bathroom in any home she had ever seen, including state-of-the-art appliances. She couldn't imagine how they got all that in here.

Bonnie fixed them all great salads and ham sandwiches on fresh wheat bread.

Bonnie and Duster and Dawn tried their best to explain time travel and different timelines to her over lunch. But the harder they tried, the more confused Sherri felt. She never considered herself a dumb person. She had four different degrees, after all and had written three best-selling books on home renovation, but all this talk about time travel just seemed to make her mind feel like it didn't work.

Yet she had experienced time travel. That fact her mind would not allow her to discount.

So all she kept focusing on was getting the chance to see her wonderful mansion in its original glory. Now that she sort of understood that might actually be possible, she wanted to pack a camera and other things to take notes, but Bonnie and Duster said it would be too dangerous. She could go back in time as often as she wanted, since only two minutes and fifteen seconds passed in her time here. And she could take notes in regular notebooks, but they didn't want her taking back modern equipment for fear it would fall into the wrong hands.

"Imagine if I had had cameras and other modern stuff with me when I fell off that horse and broke my neck last time back?" Duster had said.

So she understood. They had to go and blend in completely. She figured that was going to be one of the tougher things, even though she knew a lot about the people and habits of the time period from her research on homes.

By the time they were packed again and back in the big crystal cavern, Sherri was just as terrified as before. But now the terror had a little excitement mixed with it.

This time though, Duster met them with horses and supplies as he had planned to do the first time.

From there, they had set out quickly and it had taken them two long, somewhat grueling days and one night to get from that mine to Boise. She had rode and walked, mostly walked, the first day, since it had been some time since she had done any riding. Sore didn't begin to describe how she felt that first night.

By the time she managed to get into a hot bath in her wonderful sixth floor suite in the Idanha Hotel on the second night, she could barely feel parts of her body and her mind had completely shut off.

She was fairly certain she fell asleep in her bath because one moment the water was almost too hot, the next her skin was pruned, the water cold and dirty from all the grime of two days on horseback.

Somehow, after using cold water from the tap to rinse off, she had managed to get dressed in running shorts and a t-shirt and crawl into the most comfortable featherbed she had ever felt and snuggle down under a quilt that felt like a hug from a good friend.

The sun starting to clear the mountains woke her after what seemed like only a moment.

She splashed cold water on her face, combed her hair and put it up, and then got into the only dress that she had at the moment, including the somewhat painful woman's underwear of the time. Bonnie and Dawn promised shopping later in the day, since they said they might want to spend a couple months in the past before heading back.

Now that she was awake, she actually took a few minutes to admire her wonderful suite.

The room was named Avalanche Creek and it consisted of three rooms. One was a large living room area in the corner of the building with a round corner portico extended out where the corner would have been. The ceilings were impossibly high at twelve feet for the entire suite and electrical lights in sconces were spaced along the wall.

Electricity was new at this point in hotels. Only the top and most modern hotels had it and clearly this hotel had planned for it from the start.

A Queen Anne desk sat in one corner and a large overstuffed cloth couch and three overstuffed armed chairs surrounded a center area in front of a massive stone fireplace. All had a light brown and gold pattern to them that matched the wood and stone tones of the room.

Area carpets covered parts of the polished dark mahogany floors and thick drapes hung beside each window with smaller privacy drapes on the lower window panels. Since she was on the top floor of the tallest building in Boise, she doubted even the privacy drapes were necessary.

The morning light was wonderful in the room, giving it a faint tint of orange. She flat hated mornings, but today she was enjoying this one. It seemed her internal clock had shifted to this time, thankfully.

She could live in this room for years, she had no doubt.

She had lived in Boise off and on her entire life and had no idea of the glory of this old hotel. Someone a few years back had bought it and restored it. She hoped they did even half of the details she could see here. She would have to check it out when she got home.

The bedroom was dominated by high windows, another stone fireplace, and a dresser and a nightstand with a large round mirror over it.

The bathroom was much smaller. It had the large claw-footed tub against one wall and a brand new toilet with the tank halfway up the wall and a long brass pull chain. There was also a cast-iron sink and maple vanity stand.

The windows didn't come all the way down the walls, allowing for privacy from the outside while leaving the curtains open.

Large fluffy brown bath towels were stacked near the sink on a low table, along with a few washcloths and hand towels.

There was no hot water from the one faucet in the tub, so last night she had had to wait for the staff to bring her up buckets of hot water for her bath. But clearly, for 1902, this bathroom was top of the line. She had no idea what Duster was paying for this suite. At some point she would have to talk with him about money. She had some he had given her in her saddlebag, along with some gold.

After she finished dressing, she wished she had thought of bringing some sort of watch. She was to meet Bonnie and Duster and Dawn in the dining room just after 6 a.m. for breakfast. She had made a crack about yet another early morning, but at this point she didn't mind at all. The night's sleep in that wonderful bed had refreshed her and she was hungry.

She locked her room and with her sun hat in her hand, headed for the dining room, enjoying every architectural detail of the hotel on the way down the grand staircase.

She was three steps inside the big, beautiful dining room before she realized Bonnie and Duster and Dawn weren't there yet.

Now what was she supposed to do?

The reality of actually being in the past suddenly hit her.

Over the past two days Bonnie and Dawn had explained to her what it was like being a woman of means in 1902. Sherri had thought she understood them, both the advantages and the really bad sides of it.

But now standing here, alone, in this mostly empty dining room, she didn't know what to do.

The room looked as if it had just opened for breakfast, so chances are she was just early. She glanced back through the door of the dining room at the grand staircase, but no sign of Bonnie or Duster or Dawn.

The reality of actually being in the past suddenly hit her.

"May I help you?" a waiter with bright eyes and a dark moustache said, bowing slightly.

"I am to meet three friends here in a moment," she said, proud that her voice didn't crack.

He nodded and led her to a table with a white tablecloth and a red flower in a crystal vase in the center. He held her chair while she sat and she thanked him.

"May I get a glass of water while I wait?" she asked. "With ice, please."

He nodded and smiled. "Certainly."

Bonnie had told her that people of means asked for ice, even in the heat of the summer. It was more expensive, but a status thing.

With that the waiter left, leaving her sitting there alone.

In 1902.

What had she gotten herself into?

She had no idea what to do next. She understood how to eat in this time period, but she didn't understand if she should take her napkin and place it on her lap or not now, or wait.

And she had no idea what to do with her hat. Not a clue.

She forced herself to take a deep breath and calm down.

As Bonnie had said earlier, her actions in this timeline would have little to no effect unless she did something major. So she could relax.

Another deep breath and she could feel herself getting comfortable in the wonderful, high-ceilinged room. The ceiling had to be almost twenty feet overhead, with large chandelier light fixtures hanging down about ten feet. They were not turned on since so much natural light was flowing through the huge windows. The room almost felt as if she was eating on a grand patio.

The tops of the windows had been lowered to allow a breeze in from the cool morning air. The massive rock fireplace that filled one corner of the room didn't have a fire in it, but she imagined it could keep the room very warm in the winter.

She glanced at the two men in front of one window and then the older couple sitting against the back wall near the door. Then she glanced at the solo man sitting directly across the room from her.

She froze and just stared at him.

Never in her memory had she seen a man so handsome. He had dark hair and was clean-shaven. He wore an expensive dark suit with a vest and silk shirt under it.

And he had the most amazing green eyes and smile.

He was smiling at her.

She was just staring at him and he was smiling at her.

Oh, no, she was attracted to a guy who had been dead for half a century and he was smiling back at her.

Now what was she supposed to do?

She couldn't pull her gaze away and even in 2017 staring like she was doing would be considered rude. More than likely in this time it was almost a cardinal sin.

She could feel her cheeks flushing red, but she just couldn't look away or calm her racing heart.

What was happening to her?

He nodded and then with a smile looked down at his newspaper as his breakfast as served.

She still flat couldn't take her eyes off of him. She needed to get a grip because she was fairly certain that walking across the dinning room and sitting on his lap would be frowned on.

Wow, she had had a few crushes on men in the past, but never one at first sight like this and almost always when she had been drinking. Her work had never really allowed her to get too attached to anyone.

And there sure was no way she could get attached to a man in 1902.

Could she?

But she was. Oh, shit.

"Up early I see," Bonnie said, smiling as she and Duster approached the table. Duster wore his normal suit and black jeans and had his long oilcloth coat and hat on.

Duster held the chair for Bonnie and she said, "Well thank you, kind sir."

Duster laughed, then turned to give his hat and coat to the waiter.

"Don't you just love the past?" Bonnie said, taking her napkin and smoothing it over her lap and indicating Sherri should do the same.

"My hat?" Sherri asked, showing them her hat.

Duster offered to take it as Dawn came in and joined them.

Dawn handed Duster her hat as well and he took both of them to the waiter to hang up.

When Duster came back and sat down, Sherri allowed herself to glance in the direction of the man across the room. He was reading his newspaper and his face was hidden as he ate.

She felt a pang of disappointment and shook that off as Bonnie asked her about her suite and the wonderful conversation over breakfast went from there.

Sherri was about halfway through her wonderful eggs, ham, and fried potatoes when the man across the way stood, folded his newspaper, put on his hat, and strode toward the door.

He had to walk fairly close to them, but his gaze seemed to be focused on the door.

Again her breath caught. He was in even better shape than she had imagined, and his clothes fit him perfectly. He had to be the most alluring man she had ever seen.

He got even with their table, glanced at her, smiled, tipped his hat, and kept walking.

Again Sherri could feel her face grow pink as she smiled back and nodded in return.

Should she have done that?

Was that too forward for this time period?

In all her research on people's lifestyles and how they lived and the homes they lived in, she never once thought to learn about dating or courting, or whatever it was called at this point.

As the stranger vanished out of the door, she almost jumped to her feet and ran after him. She couldn't let the one man she had really, really been attracted to in her lifetime just vanish like that.

"Handsome man, huh?" Duster asked as he kept eating.

"He is," Sherri said. "Do you know him?"

"What did I miss?" Bonnie asked, glancing over her shoulder at the now empty doorway.

"Yeah," Dawn said, "What happened?"

"His name is Carson and he lives around here somewhere," Duster said, smiling. "I don't know his last name. I've only played a little poker with him this summer, but I've seen him at other times in the past from a distance."

Sherri nodded and stared at her food, relieved. At least he wasn't traveling through. She might have a chance to see him again.

"This is only your third day in 1902 and you're already hustling men," Dawn said, smiling. "Wow, cousin, that's some fast moves."

"Never could handle those modern ones," Sherri said, giving Dawn a wink. "Figured a dead one was safe."

"He looked far from dead to me," Duster said, shaking his head.

"I agree with that," Sherri said.

CHAPTER TWELVE

August 5, 1902
A mile outside of Boise, Idaho

CARSON MANAGED to not allow himself to walk back into that dining room and sit down with the four of them and tell them who he actually was. He just wasn't sure if he did that, it would mess up Duster and Bonnie allowing him to use the mine for his research.

He just didn't know enough about time travel and timeline travel to understand the repercussions. He was going to need to think it all through.

But he had no doubt he was going to see them again, since the wonderful woman he was so attracted to was in the process of remodeling his home in 2017. At least they had the same taste in homes.

Somehow, he managed to get his supplies and get back to his home before it got too hot. He doubted they would come out here today to look around because they had supplies and clothing to get, which meant a day of shopping. None of them would be up for a mile ride out Warm Springs Avenue in the heat after that.

That gave him a day to try to figure out what he was going to do.

And he honestly had no idea.

He got Sandy brushed down and in the stable. Then he made himself a glass of iced tea and went out to his back porch with a notebook to try to get his thoughts together.

The cottonwood trees shaded the back porch and the Boise River below the bluff flowed lazily past. Birds were still chirping in the trees, not yet settled in for the hot day.

His back porch was painted white with a thick white railing all the way around between massive mahogany posts that held up the rooms above, the same look as the front porch. Only this porch ran the entire length of the back of the mansion and wrapped slightly around the left side.

He had one overstuffed chair out here with an end table beside it. He had really never invited anyone to see his home before, so no one had sat out here with him.

But right now he wanted Sherri Edwards to be sitting here beside him. In all his years he had never felt like that about a woman. Even the women he met and sometimes married in Europe on different trips into the past. The women had all been nice and one named Gwen he had met and married and lived decades with on six different trips before deciding that was enough. He loved her, and sometimes missed her, but he knew she would always be there in any of the timelines.

But Sherri Edwards from 2017 was different. She was from his own time. That changed everything. No do-overs if he screwed this up.

That thought just scared the hell out of him.

He sipped on the cool, unsweetened iced tea and stared out over the river. So was he going to ask them to see his home?

Was he going to admit to Duster and all of them who he was?

He sat there, staring out over the river, thinking, until his lack of iced tea and the warming heat drove him back inside for the day without an answer.

CHAPTER THIRTEEN

August 5, 1902
Idanha Hotel, Boise, Idaho

SHERRI KEPT HOPING as they were out shopping, and then at lunch and dinner that she would see the handsome man named Carson, but he was nowhere to be found.

But she enjoyed the shopping with Dawn and Bonnie and by the time the day was finished, they all had good wardrobes.

That evening Dawn and Bonnie and Sherri sat in Bonnie's suite talking, letting the cooling evening breeze in. Duster was downstairs playing poker so they talked about everything just as if they were sitting in a lunch in Boise.

It felt surreal to Sherri, but Bonnie and Dawn were so comfortable, they made her feel comfortable as well.

Finally Sherri asked the question she had wanted to ask Bonnie.

"How long have you lived?"

Bonnie laughed. "Since we went to school together, I assume you don't mean in our modern time."

"How many times back here?" Sherri asked, almost afraid of the answer.

"Stopped counting a modern year ago or so," Bonnie said, "at about a thousand trips back. Some were short, like that first one we took when Duster didn't show, many other trips I died of old age in the past, usually in San Francisco."

"Duster always with you?"

Bonnie shook her head and laughed. "For the first thousand years or so we stuck together, continuing to work out the math of it all, but after that we now mostly go different directions. He likes playing Marshal up here in the Wild West and I like the luxury of San Francisco living."

"For the first thousand years?" Sherri asked, stunned.

Dawn laughed. "Stunned me as well when I first asked that question, but I'm now past that many years as well."

"You don't look a day over eight hundred," Sherri said, trying to think of something intelligent to say.

"Well, thank you, I think," Dawn said, laughing.

"How do you even stay sane?" Sherri asked. "Or remember anything."

"We have our work," Bonnie said. "That's what keeps us sane."

Dawn nodded.

"And because only two minutes and fifteen seconds actually pass," Bonnie said, "it puts things in perspective quickly. The modern time is what is important. We are just visitors in these timelines."

Sherri made herself take a deep breath. "So we can stay here and have families and die of old age and return as normal to the cave?"

Both Dawn and Bonnie nodded.

"Thinking of that hot guy from breakfast?" Dawn asked, grinning.

"Actually, I am," Sherri said. "How exactly would that work?"

"Unless all four of us wanted to remain for a long time back here beyond our planned two months, it wouldn't," Dawn said.

"Because all of us came back together?" Sherri asked.

Bonnie nodded. "As you saw when Duster didn't show, if the machine gets unplugged, we all return."

"So if I came back alone and met him," Sherri asked.

"Then you could marry him," Dawn said, "have kids, grand kids, grow old, and die."

"And when you died," Bonnie said, "you would end up in the cave just two minutes and fifteen seconds after you left, but with the memories of the full lifetime with him."

"And then you could go back again, meet him, and spend another lifetime," Dawn said.

"Wow," Sherri said, sitting back, trying to get her mind around what she had just heard. It all seemed impossible. And she would think it a drunken illusion if she wasn't actually sitting in 1902.

"Caution on having children back here," Bonnie said. "Medical practices are not what you call good."

Sherri glanced at Dawn and then Bonnie and didn't say anything.

Clearly that warning was coming from experience.

"So the kids vanish when you vanish?" Sherri asked.

"Nope," Dawn said. "What you do here in this timeline changes it. We are actually in this timeline, remember?"

"And changing it is bad?"

Bonnie shook her head. "Nothing is harmed. Our timeline remains the same for the most part. Not always, but for the most part."

"There's a story there, isn't there?" Sherri asked.

"We'll tell you about how we built Monumental Lodge at some point," Dawn said, smiling.

Sherri was stunned. That lodge had always been on the edge of the Idaho wilderness. She had heard so much about it, but never had the chance to get up there.

Bonnie waved her hand. "Far too long and too complex a story and I plan on taking a bath and being in bed before Duster gets back from the poker room."

Dawn and Sherri laughed and stood and said goodnight. They planned to meet at six a.m. for breakfast again. Sherri borrowed a small watch from Bonnie and outside Bonnie's door, Dawn said goodnight and went one way, Sherri the other to their corner suites.

This time Sherri decided on a cold bath since she had been hot most of the day. She had only been in the past for three full days now and had met the man of her dreams.

Not sure how that was possible or what to do about it, but after what Bonnie said, at least she had some options.

She still had no idea how to meet the man, but she had a few months this time back, and hundreds of other trips as well if she needed them.

She once again crawled into the wonderful featherbed and with one last thought of a handsome man named Carson, she fell asleep.

CHAPTER FOURTEEN

August 6, 1902
Idanha Hotel, Boise, Idaho

CARSON DECIDED that he needed to see Sherri Edwards again before she and Duster and Bonnie showed up at his home. He wasn't honestly sure what kind of cover story Duster and Bonnie and Sherri would come up with to knock on his door, but more than likely it would be a good one.

And he had a hunch they would be riding out his way today.

Last evening he had sat and thought back over every detail about how Bonnie and Duster had told him about the mine. It was a lot of years ago in his life, centuries back, so the memory had grown fuzzy.

He did remember they had approached him with Dawn and Madison, two of the most respected historians he had ever heard about.

Duster said they had read his doctorial thesis on World War I and had researched him and had said they could help him add in the details he was missing when he published books on the topic and the time period.

They hadn't said how at the time.

The fall before he had just taken a professor's job at the university in Boise, mostly so he could write that first book between classes. He had been stunned they even knew him in any way. Dawn said she was the one who had run across his thesis work and since he was local, she thought he would be a good choice to help.

He learned later that they had helped others. But he hadn't known about Sherri and he had no idea what that meant at all.

Was it possible that they knew him from here in 1902 before they asked him to go to the crystal cave?

Then how did he get here in the first place?

That seemed like a nasty loop of some sort and the math of that was far, far beyond him.

But he was worried that if he didn't introduce himself to them, he wouldn't be back here in a lot of different timelines, or if he did introduce himself, the same thing would happen.

As with most timelines, decisions like that caused other timelines to break off.

And all of that was complicated by his desire to meet Sherri Edwards and get to know her.

In all his many trips into the past, he had always prided himself on being slow and steady and sure of his actions. Suddenly he felt uncertain and actually afraid of a decision.

That was not like him at all.

So finally he decided to just play along and see where it led.

He saddled up Sandy before the sun broke over the hill and while the sky was still red with the sunrise. He left her at the stable behind the Idanha Hotel about fifteen minutes before six in the morning.

The large double doors to the restaurant were still closed, so he picked up a paper and stood against a column reading it while watching the stairs.

He couldn't believe how nervous he felt waiting for her to come down those stairs. He almost felt like a stalker. A time-traveling stalker, but still a stalker.

The restaurant doors opened at six and he went in and sat at the same table he had been at the day before.

About ten minutes later, Dawn and Sherri came down the stairs together, laughing at something. Both were dressed in summer dresses and looked radiant. Sherri had on a light blue dress and a matching blue floppy summer hat with a lighter-blue ribbon around the top. She moved as if she had always worn clothes from 1902.

Had she been coming back to the past before now? He doubted it from her reaction yesterday being alone. More than likely she was just relaxing and what he was seeing now was the real woman.

His breath caught and his stomach tightened up as he watched her walk across the big lobby and toward the restaurant doors. Her smile was radiant and clearly she was starting to enjoy being in the past. He had no idea who she really was except for what little he could remember from the newspaper article about her remodeling his home in 2017. And that was damn little.

They sat at the same table as yesterday and as Sherri got seated, she looked up and saw him.

He smiled at her and nodded.

Her eyes went round, her smile froze, and he could see her blush.

She quickly nodded back and then looked down at her napkin.

At that moment Duster and Bonnie joined them, so Carson went to reading his paper, blocking most of his face from them with the paper until his breakfast came.

As he laid down his paper, he caught her looking at him. She smiled, this time clearly not startled at seeing him, and he smiled back, holding her gaze.

More than anything in the world he wanted to just stand up and go introduce himself. But he just didn't dare.

At least not yet.

Finally, Bonnie said something and Sherri turned to answer her and Carson was set free from her long enough to focus on his breakfast.

He finished ahead of them and had no idea how to introduce himself to Sherri without telling Bonnie and Duster who he was, so he just folded up the newspaper and headed for the door, giving her another nod and smile as he did.

He sure wished he knew the math of all this to know what to do.

Decision points. Wasn't that what caused so many timelines?

She smiled back and luckily, neither Duster nor Bonnie saw him leave. But the morning had only made his desire to meet Sherri even stronger, if that was possible.

And he had no doubt that Duster and Bonnie and Dawn and Sherri were all headed for his home at one point or another. They would have no way of knowing he owned the place. He had left no evidence behind, including any pictures of him or even his first name on any deed. He had signed everything just Edwards.

So they had come here to meet the mysterious Edwards who killed himself in two months.

Weren't they going to be in for a surprise.

Around town he was known as Carson, not Edwards. He had always figured it was better to not let the people around town know exactly where he lived, or just how rich he was.

Safer that way.

So he got Sandy out of the stable behind the Idanha Hotel and headed home, riding at a comfortable pace for the still moderately cool morning. The clear blue skies warned of another hot day. He better get home and make some iced tea. He had no doubt he was going to have company very, very soon.

CHAPTER FIFTEEN

August 6, 1902
Outside of Boise, Idaho

SHERRI BRUSHED a loose strand of her long black hair out of her face and tucked it back under the comb holding her hair under her sun hat. She just stared at the beautiful mansion sitting back in the oak trees like she had seen a ghost.

The front porch white railings spanned between the polished mahogany columns that shined with a gleam she had only dreamed about. A simple chair sat on the porch next to a small table to hold drinks. The owner of this home must have sat there just as she had imagined doing on her porch.

The smooth river-stone walkway that led from the dirt Warm Springs Avenue up to the house seemed far wider than she had ever imagined. And the tan and brown patterned drapes that she could see through the huge windows hung perfectly.

The entire mansion was shaded by huge old oak and cottonwood trees, giving the grounds a feeling of a southern plantation. She could see through the trees and past the main building and carriage house and stable to the Boise River beyond down the bluff.

If not for the different forms of trees and stone, she could have been standing in the Deep South looking at a wonderful mansion.

She had seen pictures of the Edwards mansion in its glory, but she could not believe it had actually existed this way. The mansion was exactly how she hoped to have it look once again when she finished the remodeling in 2017.

Yet now she stood here in 1902, on the edge of the pathway leading up to the mansion, seeing her own home for herself in all its original glory, seeing it before years of neglect and abandonment had reduced it to something that really needed to be torn down, not restored.

There had been many times over the few months fighting the ghost that she had regretted the impulsive buy of the old mansion just because it had her family name attached. No one who had lived in it had actually been a relative, but in her haste to buy the old place, that hadn't mattered in the slightest.

And neither had the rumors of a ghost until she got inside and actually heard it.

Now she was going to meet the man who had killed himself and created a ghost. And she was going to meet him just two months before his death. She had no idea what she and Bonnie and Duster planned on doing. But at this point, she was enjoying the trip into the past so much, the ghost just seemed less important.

Besides, how do you stop a man from becoming a ghost? And if they did, would it help her or would she lose the mansion. Questions to ask Bonnie and Duster later.

Bonnie took Sherri's arm gently as a proper lady in 1902 would do to make sure she was all right. "Hard to imagine you are actually standing here, isn't it?"

"Impossible," Sherri said. She had been in the past for three long days now and it still seemed far too much to believe.

"Not impossible," Duster, said, coming back from securing the horses to a tree near the road. "You are actually here. You want to pinch her, Bonnie, and prove it?"

Bonnie glanced over at Duster with a look that only a wife can give a husband as Sherri laughed.

"If seeing Silver City before it became a ghost town and the two-day painful horseback ride here to Boise didn't convince me, no amount of pinching is going to do it. And that's not to mention just how uncomfortable these dresses are."

"Good point," Duster said, smiling.

At the Idanha Hotel, Dawn had had to help Sherri get into her cotton summer dress of light blue before breakfast. The women in this time period really wore a lot of clothes as far as Sherri was concerned, far more than was needed for a hot August day. She had a small chest, so she had opted to not go with the bra that felt more like a prison device, but the dress had forced her to wear petticoats.

When she had looked in the mirror, she thought she ended up looking pretty darned nice. And she was glad she did because that hot guy named Carson had been in the dining room again. She couldn't believe how hard she had fallen for a man in 1902, someone she knew nothing at all about.

But with luck, she would find out more.

She just didn't know how yet.

Duster took off his wide-brimmed cowboy hat and wiped the sweat off his forehead before putting it back on. He had on his brown oilcloth duster. Under the duster he had on a thin silk shirt and black jeans.

"Are we going to stand out here or go in?" Duster asked. "Not getting any cooler. I'm starting to think Dawn had the right idea by staying back in the hotel."

Bonnie laughed. "Give Sherri a minute. This is why she came here."

Sherri just kept staring at the wonderful mansion, memorizing every detail. Somehow she would beat the ghost and have her home look like this.

Finally she turned to Bonnie and Duster. "I'm a reporter doing an article for a few different New York magazines on the great mansions of the West, right?"

Bonnie nodded.

Sherri took a deep breath and indicated that Duster should lead the way along the path toward the home.

Her home in 2016.

If she could just beat the damn ghost.

PART TWO
Meeting the Ghost

CHAPTER SIXTEEN

August 6, 1902
Outside of Boise, Idaho

CARSON WATCHED from the shadows back in his home out the front window as Bonnie and Duster and Sherri stood at the end of his long walk, talking and staring at the home. Dawn must have stayed back in town. He didn't blame her. The day was getting very warm.

Even from this much distance, he was still attracted to Sherri. How was that even possible? He had lived for so many hundreds of years, been with his share of women, but never once felt like this.

Finally, the three turned and started up the walkway toward his front door, Duster leading.

Carson's stomach clinched into a fist.

It was now or never.

And more than likely, if he didn't tell them who he really was, spending any real time with them now would cause Bonnie and Duster to recognize him in 2017.

So he could hide and pretend he wasn't home, or he could face them and take the chance.

Or he could tell them the truth.

If it wasn't for his attraction to Sherri, he would hide.

He heard their steps on his wooden front staircase and then knocking at the front door.

They were the first people to visit his home since the last of the construction workers left twenty years ago. He was proud of this place, and clearly Sherri, a woman he was attracted to beyond words, wanted to see his home as well.

Screw it. He was going to go for it.

He went to the front door and opened it, swallowing all his fear and putting on his best smile.

Duster was standing there, looking slightly stunned as Carson opened the screen door and stepped outside, letting the screen close behind him.

All three of them seemed stunned to see him.

And he didn't dare look at Sherri yet.

"Hello, Duster," Carson said, extending his hand and shaking Duster's hand.

"Carson," Duster said, nodding and shaking his hand. "I didn't know this was your place."

"Better to keep how much money I have secret from the likes of poker players like you," Carson said.

Duster laughed and turned slightly.

"This is my wife, Bonnie,"

Carson took her offered hand and bowed slightly. "An honor."

"Thank you," Bonnie said.

"And this is our good friend, Sherri Edwards," Duster said.

Carson turned to Sherri and could hardly breathe. He was close to her and looking into her dark eyes. He could tell she was shocked and blushing. He at least knew she was coming, but if she was as attracted to him as he was to her, she was going to be lucky to even nod.

She extended her hand and he took it. Her skin was smooth, firm, and sent electrical shocks through his body.

He managed to bow slightly without taking his gaze from her wonderful eyes. "An honor. I had been hoping to meet you after seeing you at breakfast. I never expected you to come calling."

Duster chuckled lightly.

Bonnie said, "Ms. Edwards is a writer doing articles on western mansions for a number of New York magazines."

"I am honored," Carson said, finally letting her hand go, even though he did not want to. "Would you like to see the inside after I get us all some iced tea?"

"I would love that," Sherri said, her voice surprisingly level and her smile real.

He held the massive wood and stained glass door for them, and all three of them barely got three steps into his entry parlor before stopping and staring at the grand staircase curving up to the left and the wonderful craftsmanship of the wood and the amazing crystal chandelier he had imported from Europe.

The stairs were a polished mahogany with an ornate carpet runner going up the middle of them. The ceiling in this front area was a good twenty feet in the air. It didn't echo because of the long drapes hanging beside the front windows on either side of the large front door.

He seldom came into the mansion this way, so it was nice to see the effect it had on others.

All three of them were just staring, mouths open.

"This is amazing," Sherri said, clearly breathless.

"Thank you," he said. "It's a surprisingly comfortable home to live in as well. Let's have tea on the back porch before the grand tour."

He turned to Duster. "You might want to bring the horses around to the back away from the road."

Duster nodded and went back out the front door.

Carson led the two women past the staircase, through a dining area and then past the large kitchen to his back porch. He didn't look back at Sherri at all, even though he wanted to.

He got his guests settled on the back porch on chairs he had taken out of storage earlier for just this moment. The back porch overlooked the wide back lawn and the river below and could steady the nerves of just about anyone. He was going to need it because he was about as nervous as he had ever been in his life.

Not even dating in high school had got him this worked up and scared. You would think after living for almost eight hundred years, he would have gotten past this sort of thing.

Duster tied up the horses to one side of the house and joined them on the back porch as Carson went inside to get the tea.

He had the tea all ready, and ice chips in the icebox, but for the few minutes he was in the kitchen he could hear them whispering. He smiled at that. He could only imagine what they were saying.

He served them all iced tea in a crystal pitcher set with real ice, which both Bonnie and Duster looked at with puzzlement, but said nothing. He knew for a fact they were wondering exactly how he got ice on a warm day in August without even being away from them for more than a few minutes to pour the tea.

In this time period, ice was usually stored in huge chunks in a basement icehouse-like room that took time to go to and chip off ice. Wouldn't they be shocked to learn he had a small ice machine in his hidden basement.

Sherri was doing everything in her power to not look at him, which he felt was funny. He caught her eye and each time she would look quickly away.

She was as attracted to him as much as he was to her, of that there was no doubt.

But he also knew she was now worried about his coming death in September.

He sat down facing the three of them, his back to the river and the beautiful scene that had caused him to build this mansion in this location in so many timelines.

Duster had taken off his coat and hat while both women were enjoying the coolness of the tea, their hats still in place as was the custom of this time period. Fashions in this time in history were not pleasant for women, of that there was no doubt.

"So, you like my little home?" he asked, smiling at Sherri.

"I do," she said, nodding. "Very much. I'm so looking forward to you showing it to me."

Her voice sort of choked and more than likely she had forgotten her cover story. He could see the worry growing in her eyes. He knew that what she really wanted to know was why he would kill himself and then haunt this mansion for such a long period of time.

She said nothing more and he let the silence build.

No one seemed to know what to say and clearly Sherri was flustered.

They sat in silence for a moment, sipping on their tea.

He just needed to get this all out in the open if he was really going to get any answers about who Sherri really was. And he really, really wanted to know everything about her.

So screw it, decision time.

He was going for it.

He laughed for a moment, then he said, "Sorry, I can't take this any longer. Honest, I have no plans on killing myself on September 20th. I fake that every time I come back."

The look of shock from all three of them was priceless.

He just kept smiling and the silence was about as thick as the warming air on the hot afternoon.

"So what year did you buy this place?" he asked, turning to smile at Sherri. "I saw an article in the paper that you were remodeling it in 2017. I remember the article said we were not relatives, but shared a last name. So what can I do to help you restore this wonderful home?"

Sherri just blinked.

He smiled. He loved the shocked look on her face. Her beautiful mouth opened, then closed, then panic filled her eyes and she glanced at Duster, who was looking just as confused as Bonnie.

He smiled at Duster and Bonnie. "You recruited me in the late spring of 2017, or will recruit me as is the case from your point of view. I am hoping beyond hope that this encounter does not jeopardize that recruitment in any fashion. I assume you are back here from the late summer of 2016, right?"

Duster nodded and Bonnie just sat there staring at him.

"You mean in all your thousands of years of traveling in time," Carson said, "you never met someone you hadn't recruited yet to do research back in time?"

"Not that anyone admitted," Duster said, glancing at Bonnie.

"Dawn and Madison did in Roosevelt, remember?" Bonnie said.

"Oh, yeah," Duster said, "but they didn't tell us."

Carson laughed. "If you three hadn't come here to my home, I wouldn't have admitted it either. But I couldn't take the chance you would recognize me and then not recruit me. I figured in the end it was better to have everything out in the open."

"More than likely you are right," Duster said, nodding.

"I think we have some math to do," Bonnie said, shaking her head.

"Yeah, a lot of it," Duster said.

CHAPTER SEVENTEEN

August 6, 1902
Outside of Boise, Idaho

SHERRI JUST SAT there stunned, not only at the fantastic man sitting across from her, but at what he had said.

He was a time traveler as well.

Duster and Bonnie looked shaken to their core.

So she finally decided to stop acting like a fish-out-of-water with her mouth and ask a few questions of the handsome green-eyed man across from her.

"I bought the place in the winter of 2015," she said, answering his question from earlier, "with the intention of restoring it so it looks like this."

She waved her arm around at the beauty that surrounded her.

"But I can't get anyone to work for me because of the stupid ghost that haunts this place, supposedly the ghost of you."

Now it was Carson's turn to look surprised. "The batteries weren't supposed to last that long," he said. "They were supposed to die about the time the money I left in trust to keep this home in shape ran out so someone could buy it and keep it up. No wonder the home had gotten run down."

"Batteries?" Sherri asked. "You're saying the ghost is a fake?"

"Of course," Carson said, laughing. "Ghosts don't exist."

"And neither did time travel until I came back here," she said, enjoying his laugh and smiling back. She was gaining her strength and footing with him.

"You want to see where I hid it?" he asked. "So you can fix it when you get back."

"I damned sure do," she said, standing as he did. "That stupid ghost has caused me more grief than I want to think about."

"You coming, Bonnie and Duster?" Carson asked as he led Sherri into the cooler insides of the house. "Bring your tea."

Sherri had her crystal glass of iced tea in her hand, helping her keep cool in the growing heat.

Bonnie and Duster were still just sitting, their glasses in their hands, looking totally stunned, more than likely lost in the math of the situation, if she knew them.

Maybe she was accepting Carson as a time traveler faster than they were because in thousands of years this had never happened to them before. She was still new to this insanity.

Together, she and Carson went into the front parlor, then Carson pointed to a panel up about two feet below the twelve-foot ceiling. "The ghost device is in there, disguised as an old ice box that is locked up tight. It was designed to echo through the air spaces in the walls throughout the house."

"Oh, trust me, it does," Sherri said. "Can't get a workman to stay in the building."

Carson laughed. "Sorry. I just never thought the batteries would last until 2016."

"Glad they did," Sherri said. "I wouldn't be here otherwise."

Then she realized what she had said and blushed.

"I'm really glad they did as well," he said, smiling at her.

For a moment, she thought he was going to reach out and take her hand. If he did that, she wondered if her knees would hold her up. What she wanted more than anything else was for him to just hold her and kiss her.

But sadly, he didn't take her hand. They just held each other's gaze for a moment before Duster and Bonnie came up behind them and finally broke the silence.

"Think we can talk for a bit about you being a time traveler?"

Carson laughed. "I think so. Let's go downstairs where it's comfortable and cool."

"There is no downstairs in this mansion," Sherri said, stunned. "I know, I have copies of the original plans."

She instantly realized how silly that sounded since she was standing with the original owner and builder just twenty years after he had built the place.

Carson gave her that smile that wanted to melt her into a hot puddle on the polished stone floor. "Haven't found it yet, huh?"

"Haven't been able to with your stupid ghost haunting me," she said, smiling back at him.

"I hope to do more than just haunt you," he said, smiling at her, before turning away and heading toward the kitchen area.

She just stood there, her mouth once again doing the fish-out-of-water routine until Bonnie took her arm and nudged her forward.

"Damn men can do that to you, can't they?" Bonnie whispered.

"I heard that," Duster said behind them.

"I'll see who's going to do what to whom," Sherri said softly to Bonnie and the two of them laughed all the way to the kitchen and the hidden door behind a stove that led to the secret basement.

CHAPTER EIGHTEEN

August 6, 1902
Outside of Boise, Idaho

CARSON SPENT the next two hours in his air-conditioned basement living area, flirting with Sherri and explaining to Bonnie and Duster how he had gotten to this time at this point, and how he knew about Bonnie and Duster. And how they had trained him. Or more accurately, would train him.

He had designed his hidden basement to look more like his family room in 2017 than it did in 1902. Two walls were covered in books and the floor was covered in thick area rugs. The furniture was comfortable and plain overstuffed, not really showing a time period.

The main room was about the size of a large living room, and he also had a fruit cellar and wine cellar to one side of the basement.

Outside, in a hidden shed, he had a small generator working off of a nearby artesian spring, and he had also used the cool water from it to build an air conditioner in the wall down here, vented out under the back porch.

He also had a small fridge and small ice-maker from parts and coolant he had packed into Boise with him from the old mine. The cold water from the spring helped most of it work.

The room was lit by four standing electric lamps with tan shades that gave the room a comfortable feel. He loved it in this room and spent most of the warm days in here.

He sat in his favorite reading chair facing Bonnie and Duster who were sitting on his favorite nap couch. Sherri sat on a second chair that matched his reading chair, facing him.

He never understood why he had brought that second chair down here when he built the room. No one had sat in it in thirty times building the mansion, but now he understood why. Maybe somehow he knew Sherri was coming in some strange way. She seemed to fit in the room and in the chair.

Even after two hours of talking and laughing, the attraction he felt toward Sherri hadn't dulled in the slightest. He just wanted to spend more and more time with her the better he got to know her.

"So let me get this straight," Sherri said. "In the late spring of 2017, Duster and Bonnie recruit you. Correct?"

"They will," Carson said, nodding. "In June. I studied in college and did my thesis on the time period around World War One and Europe."

"I need the exact time and date that we recruit you," Bonnie said, "and who was with us, and the story you remember." Bonnie pulled out a small notebook and pencil.

He gave her all the details, including that Dawn and Madison were along.

"We need to make sure that happens in exactly that same way," Bonnie said to Duster and he nodded.

"So you think that might have happened naturally without us meeting here?" Carson asked.

"Had to," Duster said, "because you are here. We just want to keep the time divisions down if we can, when we can."

"So we pattern this after the way it actually happened, so nothing changes in billions more timelines," Bonnie said.

"Trust me," Duster said, "we'll be doing a lot of math on this before that day."

Sherri just shook her head and muttered something about how time travel could give her a headache.

"You're not the only one," Duster said.

Carson completely agreed with that, but was relieved that Duster and Bonnie were going to work to make sure his recruitment to time travel remained the same.

"So how does this work now?" Sherri asked. "When we go back to the mine and pull the plug on the machine, are we going to cut Carson's trip short in this timeline as well?"

Silence for a moment as the two great math brains thought it through.

Carson nodded to her. She was really, really smart, of that he had no doubt, and he liked that a lot about her.

"Interesting question," Bonnie said, "not sure if it worked that way when Dawn met Janice and Steven in Roosevelt. We would have to ask Janice and Steven. Never occurred to me to be honest."

"We're going to have to do the math on that as well to confirm it all," Duster said. "But my gut sense is that when we unplug the device, the four of us will go back to our original timeline, but the machine will still be hooked up for Carson for his timeline. We'll get to test that in September when we all head back."

"Original timelines?" Carson asked. "Are you saying I might be from another timeline?"

"More than likely," Bonnie said. "But it won't make any difference at all since the you from our timeline is sitting here with the three of us from another timeline and so on. Exactly the same people."

"No doubt that I'm going to have a headache now," Sherri said, shaking her head.

Carson had to agree with her on that. He decided the best thing to do was let the super math brains work out the details and then tell him in plain English how it worked. And clearly, the two math brains were puzzled on all this as well.

Sherri glanced at Carson, then turned to Duster and Bonnie. "So what happens if Carson doesn't leave in two months and let people think he killed himself? Will I be able to buy the house in the future?"

"Since you came from a timeline where you bought the house, then yes," Duster said and Bonnie nodded. "But better at this point to just keep everything consistent."

Carson was very glad to hear that, and he agreed that if they were going to pattern his recruitment perfectly, than he should pattern his leaving in two months as he always did. At least this time.

"So in how many timelines do Carson and I both exist?" Sherri asked.

Both Bonnie and Duster shrugged.

"More billions and billions and billions than I want to try to think about," Duster said. "In some you meet, in some you don't."

"Now I am one hundred percent convinced I have a headache," she said.

Carson just smiled. "Put it to you this way. In this timeline we met. Which means we will meet in many billions of other timelines. And I like the sound of that, to be honest."

"As do I," she said, blushing slightly and holding his gaze.

CHAPTER NINETEEN

August 6, 1902
Outside of Boise, Idaho

SHERRI WAS STUNNED when Carson suggested that they go get Dawn, have a short lunch in town, and return to let him cook them dinner, so they could eat in air-conditioned comfort. She loved the idea.

It meant she could spend a lot more time today with him.

"And besides," Carson said. "It's almost lunch time and I still haven't shown you my home, which I can do after lunch. And feel free to bring with you modern clothes for a comfortable afternoon and evening."

"Shouldn't you be worried about other guests dropping by?" Sherri asked.

Carson laughed. "You are the first guests in thirty-one times building this mansion that I have ever had. I lived here twenty years each time."

Now Sherri was really, really stunned. She just stared at the handsome man and he smiled back at her.

"In fact," he said, "you and Bonnie are the first two women to ever set foot in this mansion."

Sherri flat didn't know what to say about that.

Bonnie said simply, "Wow."

Bonnie and Duster both agreed to lunch and dinner and fifteen minutes later the four of them were riding at a comfortable pace back into Boise along the rutted and dusty Warm Springs Avenue in the mid-day heat. The road wound along the bluff over the river and was mostly shaded by tall oak and cottonwood trees. That helped a lot with the heat and a slight breezed helped more. But still Sherri felt she was far, far overdressed for the weather.

Sherri mostly rode beside Carson and at one point Carson pointed down toward the river. "This is where the Broadway Bridge will be built and the swamp area to the west will eventually be the Boise University Campus. They have already built one building there."

Bonnie and Duster nodded, since they clearly had been out here in the past before. Sherri just shook her head, trying to imagine all the modern buildings superimposed over the mostly empty landscape.

Back in the hotel, Duster and Carson got them a table in the dining room while Bonnie and Sherri went upstairs to freshen up and tell Dawn a little of what happened.

They both went to Dawn's room and found her sitting at the desk in shorts and a Cal Tech t-shirt. Her room had kept its coolness so far and she had the drapes pulled to block any direct sunlight.

"Time to get dressed," Bonnie said. "We have a lunch date."

"With whom?" Dawn asked as she headed for the bedroom.

"You know the hot guy at breakfast?" Sherri asked.

"Carson?" Dawn asked, looking at Sherri and smiling. "Seriously?"

"He ended up owning the Edwards Mansion," Sherri said.

"And he's from 2017," Bonnie said. "We haven't recruited him yet in our time."

Dawn now looked like a fish out of water.

"And he has a hidden air-conditioned basement," Sherri said, "where he wants to serve us dinner tonight."

Dawn just shook her head and finally closed her mouth.

"This is like you meeting Janice and Steven in Roosevelt," Bonnie said. "He didn't want to tell us who he was, but by going to his mansion, we forced him to reveal himself."

"He didn't dare take a chance," Sherri said, "that Bonnie and Duster would recognize him in 2017 when they recruit him."

"So he doesn't kill himself in two months?" Dawn asked as she stripped down and Bonnie headed for the bathroom to freshen up.

"Nope," Sherri said. "And the ghost was fake, battery run, not meant to last as long as it did."

"Wow, just wow," Dawn said. "I decide to stay in the hotel one morning and look what I miss. So you jumped his bones yet?"

Sherri pretended to be insulted. "No, how dare you. I'm a lady."

Dawn just snorted.

"She wanted to," Bonnie said from the bathroom.

Sherri laughed. "Got that right. And the day is still young."

"Well," Dawn said, "as the old saying goes, when the mansion is rockin', the other guests get walkin'."

CHAPTER TWENTY

August 6, 1902
Outside of Boise, Idaho

CARSON SAT next to Sherri and completely enjoyed the lunch in the hotel dining room with the other four. He was so glad now that he had decided to just come clean to them, since both Bonnie and Duster were not worried about the implications of him doing that at all.

As Duster had said during lunch, "In some timelines you take this route, in others you decide to continue to hide from us. Decisions are just decisions we live with."

After lunch, through the growing heat, the five of them rode back out to the mansion. Carson again tried to stay close to Sherri and they laughed and talked about different things along the way.

For the very first time in any trip into the past, he felt comfortable with others. And he felt really happy to have all of them in his mansion. Especially Sherri.

When they got to his home and had the horses taken care of in the stable, the women went inside and changed from their 1902 dresses to modern jeans and light blouses and tennis shoes.

Duster left on his jeans, but took off his hat and changed his shirt to a lighter dress shirt with rolled-up sleeves. Carson did the same, changing out the cowboy boots for sneakers and putting on a lighter shirt.

Sherri looked even more stunning dressed in modern comfortable clothes. She had her hair pulled back and tied and she had scrubbed her face. He could see through her light shirt that she had a sports bra on.

"Ready for a tour?" Carson asked as all five of them gathered in the kitchen. He had made glasses of iced tea for each of them to carry and because the house had been closed up for the morning, it was still moderately cool.

He started with the upstairs and the four massive bedrooms to each side of a hallway almost as wide as a regular room. He hated narrow hallways and had done that on purpose, adding some seating and bookshelves to the hallway to make it inviting at the top of the massive staircase.

Each room upstairs had high ceilings, electrical lighting he had installed himself about five years before, and 1890s period furniture. He had kept the drapes pulled closed for coolness on the tall windows.

"Any hidden rooms I'm going to find up here?" Sherri asked, smiling as she looked around with wide eyes, taking in every detail.

"Just wait and see," he said, smiling at her.

After showing them the other three bedrooms and the bathroom off the hallway, he led them into his master bedroom, the last large stained-wood door at the end of the massive hallway.

"I even made my bed this morning because I had a hunch you all were coming out this way today."

His massive master bedroom would hold three normal bedrooms, with ceilings that towered sixteen feet overhead. Three glass chandeliers hung from the ceiling, giving the room an almost daylight glow when he turned them on, even though the heavy drapes were still pulled.

He had four or five smaller reading lamps around the room and a couch and two overstuffed chairs around a coffee table in the middle of an area rug.

"Wow, this is a room," Bonnie said.

"You could run laps in here," Dawn said, shaking her head.

Two of the walls were massive bookcases that stretched up twelve feet and were filled with leather editions. A wooden ladder on a rail moved around so he could reach any of the books he wanted.

He loved this room and this library, even though he kept most of his really treasured books on the shelves in the basement.

"Now I see what you do for twenty years with no guests," Duster said.

"And play a little poker," Carson said, laughing. "But I do love to read, although many of these in here would be boring to most. Works on certain people who lived in Europe."

He then showed them his walk-in closet that was as big as some hotel rooms, and lined on all four sides with hanging clothes. Shoes lined up under the clothes and hats fit along on the shelves above.

"It is usually not this neat, and since I have never tossed away any clothes in twenty years, that's why it's full. I'm not really this much of a clothes hound."

"Wow, I would die for a closet this big," Dawn said. "I am a clothes and shoes hound and damn proud of it."

"I wondered what these two rooms was used for," Sherri said. "I just thought it was a library and a storage room, not your bedroom and closet. All the books and furniture were gone by the time I bought the place, so it was tough to tell, especially with those chandeliers."

Carson nodded. "Did you find this yet?"

He pointed to a built-in wooden bench to one side of the door into the walk-in closet. He had made it to look plain, as if just something to sit on while pulling your boots on.

"It still there," she said.

He moved over to the bench and pointed to a small polished knot in the wood on the right. "Push that."

She stepped over and pushed and the bench popped open.

She stepped back. "Wow, nifty."

Inside he kept a little money and an extra gun and some extra ammunition for his two rifles in the case downstairs.

Bonnie and Duster were just shaking their heads.

"Now push the button again," Carson said, smiling at Sherri.

She did and there was a click, but nothing happened.

Carson reached over and pulled on the lid of the bench slightly and the wall behind the bench, including the entire bench, swung open like a door.

"Now that's clever," Duster said.

Carson led them inside. The room behind the hidden door was about the size of a normal bedroom. He had shelves on both side walls holding extra stacks of money, a few stacks of gold bars and a couple bags of gold, and numbers of rifles and guns and ammunition.

There was also a chair and a reading light and a lantern and a number of books. At the end of the room a narrow staircase led down and another led up.

"All the gold and money I take back to the cavern each trip," Carson said. "I pull it all out of here, carry it up near Silver City and bury it, then dig it up when I leave. If I get killed while in Europe, there's a hidden gold stash someone might find at some point."

Duster nodded. "Looks like you are adding to the fund some."

"On the trips I make it back alive," Carson said. "I think I'm about even so far."

"How do you make all that?" Sherri asked.

"Duster will teach you," Carson said.

Duster and Bonnie both nodded.

"This is my safe room," Carson said after he clicked on the light and allowed them to look around for a moment. "Instead of fighting off someone trying to attack the place or rob it, I could just sit in here."

"Ever happen?" Duster asked.

"Not in all the time I have spent in this place," Carson said.

Duster nodded. "Boise is one of the safest places in the Old West."

"Where do the stairs go?" Sherri asked, walking over to the up staircase.

"The up staircase goes to a trap door in the roof that would allow me to get out along a ledge and into a large tree to the right of the mansion if I needed to escape for any reason like a fire or attack. The down staircase leads to a hidden door in the kitchen."

"So you could go from your room in the basement, through the kitchen and up here to your bedroom without ever going out into the larger main part of the house," Dawn asked.

"I could," Carson said, nodding, "but I like the rest of the house too much. I tend to live in most parts of this place except for the extra bedrooms. Those have never been used. I change out the sheets and quilts every five years just in case."

After that he led them back out through his bedroom and out into the book-lined hall and back downstairs. Then he showed them the main rooms downstairs before they ended up back in the kitchen.

"Amazing place," Duster said. Bonnie and Dawn both nodded.

"It is wonderful," Sherri said. "I hope I can do it justice in 2017."

"I think you can," Carson said, looking into her wonderful dark eyes.

She smiled at him. "Thanks, I'll try. If you'll help."

Carson had to admit, in all the times building this same mansion in varied timelines, and living in it for twenty years every time, he had never felt more proud of anything before.

"It would be my honor," he said.

She just blushed, which he liked a lot.

CHAPTER TWENTY-ONE

August 6, 1902
Idanha Hotel, Boise, Idaho

SHERRI COULD not believe how much had been packed into one day. This morning she hadn't even really known Carson Edwards. He was just a handsome man across the dining room from her who smiled at her.

Then discovering he was a time traveler like she was and the owner of the mansion. And that the ghost was a fake she could fix easily.

Then the wonderful lunch, the fantastic tour, and a comfortable dinner that she had helped him with. It felt so natural being in that kitchen with him beside her. They had laughed, joked, teased each other, and every time they touched, she wanted to just kiss him.

But it wasn't until after dinner when she and Carson had gone back up to the kitchen to get desserts for everyone that she couldn't take it any longer and had kissed him.

And he had kissed back.

And the warm kitchen had gotten a lot, lot warmer very, very quickly.

She wasn't sure if they lost track of time or what, but by the time that kiss broke, she had known they both wanted the same thing. The problem was 1902.

So as they both caught their breath and finished dishing up the light chocolate cake to take down to everyone, she had said to him.

"I'm alone in the Avalanche Creek suite on the sixth floor."

"Is this an invitation?"

"Damn tootin' it is," she had said, smiling at him. "I need someone to scrub my back in that big tub in my suite. Bring a change of clothes for breakfast."

"A woman who knows her own mind," he had said, smiling, then kissing and pressing his entire body against her.

He had felt wonderful. She certainly wasn't a prude, but kissing him had the excitement of a first date all over again. And she had loved it.

Now she was back in her room after another hour of conversation in Carson's basement, then a nice ride with Bonnie and Duster and Dawn into town. Carson had said he would meet them all for breakfast and they could talk about what to do next.

Sherri had gone to her room, washed the first layer of dust off her arms and face and changed into a pair of running shorts and a t-shirt with nothing on under it. She had combed her hair and pulled it back.

She had left the drapes in the big suite pulled closed while she was gone, which had kept the rooms slightly cooler than outside, but now the early evening was starting to cool down. Later on, when it got much cooler, she would open a top window on both sides of the room to let out the hot air and allow a cool night breeze to come into the room.

There was a light knock at her door and she moved to the door and said, "Yes."

"Carson," the voice on the other side said.

She opened the door, standing behind it slightly so no one in the hallway would see her shorts and t-shirt.

Carson stepped through and she pushed the door closed. He was dressed as he had been at the house in a light silk dress shirt with the sleeves rolled up and dark jeans. He had a saddlebag over his shoulder.

He dropped the saddlebag beside the door and looked at her with a look she loved. "Wow, you look great."

She held out her arms. "I dressed up for you."

He laughed and stepped toward her and kissed her, pulling her against his body.

Again, like the first kiss in his kitchen, she lost track of any sense of time.

Finally they broke the kiss and stepped back slightly, holding hands.

His face was flushed and she knew her face was as well.

"Up for a cool bath?" she asked, smiling.

"With you," he said, smiling, "I doubt any bath will be cool."

She kissed him again, then slid out of his grasp and headed for the bathroom, taking off her clothes as she went until she got to the bathtub and bent to turn on the water completely nude.

He had followed her through the bedroom and to the bathroom where he stood in the door watching, his face red, his eyes wide.

She turned to face him so he could see all of her. She loved how he was admiring her. It had been a very long time since any man had looked at her like that.

"It seems that one of us," she said, "has far too many clothes on and I don't think it's me."

By the time he had his clothes off and had joined her at the large claw bathtub, she had climbed in and was standing in the warmish water. It seemed the water tank on the roof of the building had warmed up the water some in the day's heat.

Either that or she was so sexually aroused, her body was warming the water. More than likely that was the cause.

She watched him climb into the tub, admiring his wonderful body and all his muscles. And he was clearly excited about what they were doing.

She had brought some soap from the future, so they spent the next ten minutes scrubbing each other in all sorts of ways while kissing and laughing and splashing far too much water onto the floor.

Finally, they crawled out and toweled each other dry. By that point, all Sherri wanted to do was make love to this fantastic man. So she pulled him into the bedroom, threw back the quilts and kissing, the two of them fell onto the soft featherbed.

Once again all sense of time left for her as they just seemed to fit together in more ways than she ever wanted to admit.

She had only known this man for less than a day and she was already falling head over heels for him. This was not something that had ever happened to her before.

Their first session was fast, hard, and intense. Exactly what they both needed.

Then they rested for a short time in each other's arms until he started kissing her shoulder and working his way down her body slowly, one gentle kiss at a time.

This time the lovemaking was slower.

Much slower and much, much more fun.

Afterwards, even though the room was still warm, they fell asleep in each other's arms.

For Sherri, that felt perfect.

And she didn't want to even think about a relationship with a man she barely knew as perfect. At least not at the moment.

Or all the problems the two of them being together would cause.

She just wanted to enjoy it.

CHAPTER TWENTY-TWO

August 7, 1902
Idanha Hotel, Boise, Idaho

CARSON AWOKE to some birds chirping outside the hotel window. It was still dark out as far as he could tell, and Sherri was curled with her back against him. In the light from the one lamp they had left on in the bathroom, she looked stunning. Her long black hair cascaded over her shoulders and her seemingly perfect skin was so soft to the touch, he couldn't seem to stop touching her.

They had just fit perfectly together making love as well. How was it even possible he was sleeping with a woman from the future in 1902? A woman he had only known for day? In over 800 years of living in the past, he had never felt anything like this, and honestly it scared him.

Not enough to change anything, or even want to. It was just a new and exciting fear. A fear that he wouldn't be good enough for this fantastic woman.

He stared at her for a few long minutes until she rolled over and kissed him. Before they could get started once again, she asked, "Any idea what time it might be?"

"Let me find out," he said, rolling reluctantly away from her and going to his jacket and his pocket watch. It was almost five in the morning. They needed to be dressed and downstairs in an hour for breakfast.

He turned and she was staring at him, smiling. "Anyone ever tell you how handsome you are?"

"Not in a very long time," he said, moving back over to the bed and crawling onto the bed so he could face her and look at her wonderful body as well. "But you realize that in this body I am twenty years older than I am in the future."

"We are the same age there," she said, nodding. "I like that."

"So do I," he said. "I'll have more stamina."

She laughed. "Promises, promises."

He moved against her and kissed her and thirty minutes later, after another wonderful session, they were up together, naked in her bathroom, washing up and getting ready for breakfast.

After she was mostly dressed and he was just finished pulling on his boots, she asked, "So how are we going to get downstairs?"

He laughed. "Bonnie and Duster and Dawn are three very smart people. I think we just walk down together. They won't be surprised. Would you in their position?"

She laughed and shook her head, then turned to have him help her button up her dress in the back. He loved doing that, loved watching her dress, loved being around her.

After she was ready to go, her sunhat in her hand, her long black hair up and held by two bone combs, she stood in front of him, looking completely radiant.

"Does this scare you?" she asked, her dark eyes looking very serious.

"Petrified," he said. Then he decided to be honest with her because he felt he just couldn't do anything else. "This feels very special to me and I'm deathly afraid of doing something to screw this up."

She smiled and kissed him quickly. "I feel exactly the same way."

"So two time travelers scared to death," he said.

"And not about traveling in time," she said, smiling. "And I can't believe I just said that."

He laughed and they headed to the door. She opened it, looked both ways, and the two of them stepped into the hallway.

"Back to being a lady and a gentleman in 1902," he said.

"Like being on a stage," she said as they walked slowly toward the stairs, not touching.

He most certainly wanted to hold her hand, but did not.

They made it to the main lobby and across to the now open dining room. Bonnie and Duster and Dawn were already there at the same table as lunch the day before.

They all looked up and smiled as Carson held the chair for Sherri and then went around to the other side of the table and sat down.

"Pretty nice suite, isn't it?" Duster asked, smiling.

Carson noticed Sherri blushed slightly, but was smiling.

"I honestly did not have the time or the inclination to study the room's decorations or architecture," Carson said, unfolding his napkin and smiling at Duster. "But from the large claw bathtub I did catch a glimpse of some very nice fixtures."

Duster's mouth opened, then closed and waved his hand in front of his face as if brushing away a fly. "Too much information."

At that all three women laughed and Sherri smiled at Carson, a smile that promised even more looks at her very, very, very nice fixtures.

CHAPTER TWENTY-THREE

August 7, 1902
Idanha Hotel, Boise, Idaho

AFTER BREAKFAST had been served, they talked about what to do next. Duster had tipped the staff to not seat anyone within earshot of them, so as long as they talked softly, they were safe.

Sherri, all through breakfast just kept glancing at Carson and she often caught him looking and smiling at her.

She just couldn't believe she had fallen for this man so hard. The feeling of that, as she had told him, scared her more than she ever wanted to admit being scared. The fear of something happening and losing him now would just be too much.

"Do you think I should wait until my normal departure time?" Carson asked Duster.

"I can see no reason not to," Duster said, as he worked at a piece of soft bread to dip into his eggs.

"Neither can I," Bonnie said as she gently wiped off her mouth.

"So what are you thinking of doing then?" Sherri asked, feeling worried.

"I'm just going to head back to the future and meet you there, I hope."

He looked at her and she could clearly see the worry in his eyes.

She didn't really understand the worry. Why wouldn't she want to meet him in the future.

"I like that idea a lot," Sherri said.

"But you can't meet him when you get back," Bonnie said to Sherri. "Carson won't have been recruited yet by us." Bonnie turned Carson. "When did you go through for this trip?"

"June 9th, 2017," Carson said, still looking at Sherri with the look of worry in his eyes.

Now she understood. The four of them would return just over 2 minutes after they left on September 20th, 2016. But Carson wouldn't return until June of the following year. She would have to wait for him for over eight months.

She smiled at him. "Looks like I have some time to get the mansion remodeled before you get there, doesn't it?"

He looked very relieved. Very, and he smiled in such a way that she wanted to just drag him back to her room or kiss him here in the middle of the dining room.

"That still doesn't solve what we are going to do next," Duster said. "Are we staying with our original plan or heading back early?"

Bonnie patted Duster's arm. "We're staying for a few months, dear, as we planned."

"Good," Duster said, nodding. "I want us all in the cave at the same time so Carson can see what happens when we unplug the wire for our trip. This will be a good test of the math on that."

Sherri wasn't sure what exactly Duster was talking about, but both Bonnie and Dawn were smiling fondly at him, and he wasn't noticing at all. And that made Sherri and Carson both laugh.

She had two months to spend with this wonderful man, get to know him in as many ways as possible. And study that wonderful mansion in the process.

This just might be the best two months of her life.

PART THREE
The Death of a Ghost

CHAPTER TWENTY-FOUR

September 19, 1902
Outside of Boise, Idaho

CARSON AND SHERRI watched as Bonnie and Dawn walked down the path from the mansion toward the stable. Duster was there getting the four horses ready. The September evening wasn't really warm, and Carson knew the night would end up almost cold.

"You know this isn't the end," he said, hugging Sherri's shoulder.

"I know," she said. "I know this is the beginning for us, a real beginning. But I'm going to miss the hell out of you."

There wasn't a thing he could say to that. She had to survive and wait for him for over eight months after she returned. He would return and just have the drive from the mine to Boise, so his wait to be back with her would be just hours long.

He hoped she still wanted him when he finally got there. She had promised him many times that there was no chance in hell she was forgetting him in a short eight months. "Ten months, maybe," she had said, her dark eyes boring into him, "but not eight."

They stood there in silence until Duster led the four horses out of the stable. He gave Bonnie the reins to her horse, Dawn her horse, and held the reins to Sherri's horse.

The three of them mounted up and then turned and started up toward the mansion.

The five of them had just finished a going-away dinner that he had made for them and Sherri had helped him serve it in the main dining room since it was cool enough to eat in there. That had been the first time that room and his fine china and silver had ever been used and it had been wonderful.

Now Sherri and Bonnie and Dawn and Duster would head back to town, and then leave tomorrow morning for Silver City.

He turned Sherri slowly and they walked through the mansion together, headed for the front door, his arm around her shoulders, her arm around his waist.

They fit so well together, he couldn't believe it. And she had often said the same thing.

They had talked about that a lot over the last two months, often in bed in her suite. Or sometimes in his big bed upstairs.

She belonged in this mansion as much as he did, he had no doubt. This place was home for both of them.

"You have all your sketches and plans?" he asked.

"My notebook is not leaving my person," she said. "And your plans are in my saddlebag. I want this place to look like this when you get there."

"Sorry I'm going to miss the fun," he said.

"You've built this place thirty-one times," she said, laughing softly.

"The fun would be remodeling it with you," he said, stopping by the front door and kissing her.

"How about we come back together on your next trip and both build this place for the thirty-second time," she said after they broke the kiss and he opened the large front door.

"I would love that," he said.

He walked her across the front porch and down the steps to her horse. He kissed her one more time, then helped her up and into her saddle.

"You all set?" Duster asked.

Carson nodded. "I get the body from the graveyard tonight that I dress as myself and leave hanging from the tree in the front where someone driving past will see it. My attorney is set with my estate, everything is as I planned it many times before."

"Don't forget to set that damned ghost," Sherri said, smiling at him.

"Oh trust me, I won't," Carson said, smiling back at the woman he had fallen completely in love with.

"See you in Silver City," Duster said, nodding to Carson and turning his horse away.

Bonnie and Dawn nodded and followed Duster.

"I love you," Sherri said. "You know that, don't you?"

"I know that," Carson said, walking a few steps as she started up the drive. "And you know I love you as well?"

"I do, and I'm going to be holding onto that for eight months."

She looked back at the mansion, then down at him. "And in everything I refurbish, I'll be thinking about how you built it."

"See you in Silver City," he said.

And with that he watched her ride out onto Warm Springs Avenue and turn toward Boise.

CHAPTER TWENTY-FIVE

August 7, 1902
Idanha Hotel, Boise, Idaho

SHERRI HAD wanted to spend the last night with Carson, and clearly he wanted her to spend the night with him as well. But she knew the plan they had was right in trying to keep the timelines clear. And he had so much work to do to get ready for his vanishing tomorrow.

Her biggest worry was that she would return to the present and not own the Edwards Mansion. Duster had flat told her that really wasn't mathematically possible, but they had still all decided to be safe than sorry and have Carson do everything exactly as it had been done in so many other timelines.

And in every other timeline, he had gone to a place near Silver City to bury his gold before heading to Europe. So they had decided to meet up back in Silver City in three days and all go to the mine together.

But Dawn and Bonnie had told her and Carson the story of the Monumental Summit Lodge one night over drinks in his basement. It seemed they had left to go back into time to build a huge mountain lodge up in the Thunder Mountain region of Idaho on a summit. They had built the wonderful lodge, lived in it, and then when they had returned, they remembered a timeline where it had not existed, their original timeline, and growing up with the lodge always there.

Bonnie and Duster had hired two more mathematicians to help them figure out what had happened and why they could remember two timelines.

The last thing Sherri needed was to go back and remember buying the mansion, but in her timeline she hadn't bought it, or hadn't met Carson. So both she and Carson had insisted on a lot of the safety precautions at least until they got together in the present of 2017.

The ride from the mansion back into Boise along the dirt road at night had been one of the longest and roughest Sherri had ever experienced. And her sour mood had not made it any better. She had finally met the man of her dreams, spent a wonderful two months talking and laughing with, and then she had been forced to leave him because she had met him over a hundred years in his and her past.

And that needed to be fixed in real time before anything could last. She understood it, but it sure as hell didn't help her mood.

That night she lay awake in the big featherbed of the Idanha Hotel, the same one she and Carson had first made love in two months before, hoping that somehow Carson would knock lightly on her door and come in.

She finally dozed off just before dawn and Bonnie woke her an hour later for breakfast.

She suddenly remembered clearly why she had hated mornings. In two months of waking up beside Carson, not once had she hated that, no matter the time of the day

After breakfast, with still no sign of Carson, they left on horseback for Silver City. She knew that if history followed, someone would find the body he had borrowed from the cemetery hanging in the tree right about the same time they left Boise.

Two rough and painful and hot days later they finally reached the old mining town high in the Idaho Owyhee Mountains. She barely spoke most of the way. She just didn't feel much like talking.

That night, she was so tired and sore from two days of horseback riding, she just passed out in her bed in the old Silver City Hotel. She didn't care how dirty or ratty the place looked. The old hotel was clearly past its prime.

The next morning at breakfast in the very small dining room, she still felt as if she was walking in a haze. Dawn and Bonnie and Duster seemed to be enjoying themselves, but she felt just empty.

She was picking at the pancakes she had been given for breakfast when a voice beside her asked, "Is this seat taken, Miss Sherri?"

Her head snapped around and she found herself looking into the wonderful, deep-green eyes of Carson.

He had on a fake moustache and dirty brown beard, and he wore a gray cowboy hat that looked like it had seen far better years. His jacket was dusty and soiled and his pants and boots clearly worn and old. But the smile and laugh that reached his eyes were what she loved.

"It is not taken," she said, smiling at him and indicating that he should join them.

Across the table Bonnie and Duster were both smiling. Dawn looked like she might break out into applause, but since there were others in the small dining room close by, she didn't.

As Carson sat down, he took off his hat and coat, putting both on the floor at his feet.

"Did you have a good ride?" he asked, smiling after he gave his order to one of the hotel wait staff who had been called over by Duster.

She smiled back. "I'll let you know as soon as I can actually walk normally again."

Carson laughed and she just tried to memorize every sound of it. She had loved it for months. Now she wasn't going to hear it for over eight months.

"Not used to being on horses?" he asked, clearly amused.

"Not since I had a pony at ten," she said. "Trust me, not the same thing."

Again he laughed.

And again she felt whole having him beside her, again. How was it possible that she had avoided any long-term relationships with any man for years, and now she didn't feel complete unless he was with her?

Amazing what a few months in the past could do for a girl.

After breakfast that was far too short for Sherri's tastes, Dawn and Bonnie and Duster and Sherri headed at a leisurely pace up the hill toward the old mine. The day had a bite to the air and there were very few people left in the valley, since the first snowfall was threatening.

With rests, it took them over an hour to climb the seven hundred feet up the side of the mountain. In 2016, a lot of the trees had grown back, but now the hills were mostly just covered with scrub brush and the trail was often almost overgrown.

The dress she was forced to wear with all the strange undergarments didn't make the climb any easier. Sherri was going to be very happy to get back to the old mine and be able to change into some decent modern jeans, bra and underwear, and a t-shirt.

Carson had tipped his hat to them, thanked them for the wonderful company, and left the dining room ahead of them. He had said he would take another trail around the long way and meet them at the mine. Even though there were few people living in Silver City in 1902, no point in raising any kind of question.

Sherri understood that, but the walk would have been far more pleasant with Carson along.

As they approached, single file toward the old mining shack on the mine tailings, Carson appeared from inside the old shack and smiled, pulling off his fake beard and moustache and taking off his coat.

"You look much better without the facial hair," Sherri said, smiling at him.

"Stuff itched like crazy," he said, shaking his head. "Great to be rid of it."

Duster and Bonnie and everyone checked the surrounding area for anyone too close. No one. So Duster turned the head of what looked like a skeleton key and the rock slid silently back beside the boarded up mine shaft.

Sherri was again impressed how hidden the opening really was, and how protected.

They all crowded inside and the door slid closed behind them, again making the mine outside look abandoned and boarded over.

For a moment they were in the dark, then the lights came up.

Duster and Bonnie started down the old mine tunnel side-by-side. The roof of the tunnel was a couple feet over Sherri's head and large timbers that looked old supported the rock.

Carson reached over and took Sherri's hand as they walked along behind Duster and Bonnie and Dawn.

"This place never stops amazing me," Carson said.

She squeezed his hand and agreed as Bonnie and Duster walked through what seemed to be a wall ahead of them as the mine tunnel turned to the right. They just kept walking straight ahead.

"Now that's creepy," Sherri said. "I've seen it before and it still creeps me out. Talk about ghosts. They look like ghosts walking through that wall like that."

Carson laughed and stepped into the wall and through it, pulling Sherri along before she had time to object or even think about it.

Once they were back in the big supply cavern, Dawn and Bonnie and Duster started undressing. Carson did the same, moving over to a pile of boxes on the right. It seemed they were going to have no shame, so Sherri sure wouldn't either.

"A little help with these clasps?" she said.

"Gladly," Carson said and Bonnie just smiled at Sherri as Carson undid the clasps on the back of her dress.

Sherri moved over beside Bonnie and Duster and dug out the clothes she had been wearing what seemed like a lifetime ago, undressing and dressing quickly, all the while watching Carson out of the corner of her eye.

She had never once tired in the two months of seeing him naked and now she was enjoying it one more time, making sure the memory would last her for eight long months.

After they were dressed, Duster turned and led them down another short tunnel and through another steel door and into a room that once again took Sherri's breath away.

Bonnie had said that it was almost impossible for any human mind to grasp the beauty of the crystals and the size of the cavern and Sherri felt that was right. She flat couldn't.

After a moment she turned to Carson. "One more time to make sure I have this glued to my mind, even though I have it written down in five or so places. What day do you arrive back?" she asked.

"June 9th, 2017, at about 2:30 in the afternoon," he said. "I should be at the mansion by 7 p.m. if I don't run into too much traffic along the way."

She took his hand, then reached up and kissed him.

Finally she pushed away. "That's going to have to last me for eight plus months."

"Then we had better do it once more to make sure it holds," he said, pulling her against his hard chest and kissing her again.

For what seemed like an eternity they held that kiss until finally Duster cleared his throat.

She pushed back. She looked into his green eyes and he nodded.

With that she turned, trying not to allow herself to kiss him again.

Together they all five put their hands on the small time machine. Then Duster took off one wire and around them the room really didn't change at all.

They were back in 2016.

Carson was gone.

And Sherri felt empty once again.

CHAPTER TWENTY-SIX

June 9th, 2017
Old mine above the ghost town of Silver City, Idaho

CARSON LOOKED around at the crystal cavern after Sherri and Bonnie and Duster and Dawn vanished. His wires were still hooked up to the machine and the crystal.

Duster had been right about that happening.

He put on a glove, touched the box with his bare hand, and unhooked one wire with his gloved hand. As normal, nothing seemed to change.

He carefully unhooked the other wire from the box, then the two wires from the crystal.

Then carrying his heavy saddlebags filled with money and gold, he headed for the regular cavern. He quickly stored the money, then changed back into his 2017 clothes. It had been over twenty years since he had been here, yet only slightly more than two minutes had passed. That always felt very strange and this time was no different.

He headed down the mine, setting the alarms as he went as Duster had trained him to do. He almost missed one because all he could think about was Sherri and how wonderful that last kiss had felt just a few minutes before, yet over a hundred years in the past.

But now he was going to face his biggest fear. Would she still want him after eight months?

He made sure there was no one outside the mine, then quickly opened the mine door and stepped out and let the big rock go closed behind him. The afternoon was warming up, but wasn't extremely hot yet. The air felt dry and the ghost town of Silver City far below looked like it had a few early-season visitors.

His blue Jeep SUV sat across the narrow trail in the trees near where Duster and Bonnie always parked.

Climbing in behind the wheel felt very, very strange. That last trip where he had met Sherri had been his fourth trip back today. He had only spent an hour in the mine since arriving here today, but it had been a couple hundred years of living and memory since he had last driven a car.

Duster had always said it was like riding a bike, a person didn't forget. But they could sure be rusty at the skill and that's exactly how he felt.

He sat for a moment, adjusting the air-conditioning and letting the car cool down some before carefully backing it up and then heading across the hillside on what seemed like nothing more than a goat track and then down to the valley floor and the main one-lane tourist road into Silver City.

By the time he got started back up the narrow road on the other side of the valley that crested over the summit on War

Eagle Mountain, he was feeling his driving skills coming back.

And he was relaxing a little. He didn't much like this narrow, twisting road along the tops of large cliff-like drops into the valleys below, but he had driven it a couple dozen times, so it didn't flat scare him anymore. Even after hundreds of years in the past, he remembered it well.

The road was no more than one car width wide and covered in hard dirt and loose gravel. And the road was dusty and rutted from the winter run-off. In a few places there was still winter snow drifted in under the shadows of the trees.

As he crested over the top of the summit, he could see the Treasure Valley and Boise out before him, wonderful and green compared to the brown of the mountains around him.

Sherri was there, in that valley, waiting for him. He just hoped she still wanted him.

For him, it had only been a few minutes since she left. He couldn't imagine how she was feeling right now after eight plus months of waiting.

The road made a sharp turn to the left. He knew that in another few hundred yards, the really bad narrow road would turn into a two-lane newer road made for large mining trucks. That road had been constructed a few years before to haul out loads of ore from a mine on the Treasure Valley side of War Eagle Mountain.

As Carson came around the sharp left-hand turn, his mind thinking about Sherri and her wonderful smile, a large deer stood in the road. Beside her were two small fawns.

It took him a moment to realize what he was seeing.

He wasn't going that fast but his reactions were slow as he slammed on the brakes, sliding on the dry dirt and gravel toward the doe and her fawns.

They didn't seem to be moving, so he steered toward the outside edge of the road to miss them.

The deer hesitated, clearly surprised, then finally jumped to one side and up the hill. But as they did, his front tire caught in the loose gravel along the edge of the road and yanked his Jeep hard right and out over the edge of a very, very long drop into trees and forest.

It happened so fast, there was not a thing he could do.

Nothing.

He held on as the car tipped and went over, picking up spinning speed as it tumbled down the hill.

His world spun over and over as the car just rolled and bounced down the steep slope.

He had no idea how many times it tumbled before it hit something very hard.

And then there was nothing.

The next thing he realized, he came to, still strapped into his seat. The car was lying on the passenger side and smashed up so much it didn't even much seem like a car.

The engine was ticking from heat, but off. And he could smell gas.

Glass had shattered everywhere and through the smashed and broken and much narrower windshield he could see down the valley. Clearly he hadn't rolled all the way to the bottom, for as much as that was going to help him now.

Blood was running off his forehead. He could tell he had broken arms and he could no longer feel his legs at all.

He tried to take a deep breath and screamed in agony and everything again went quickly black.

He came back awake at some point. He had no idea how much longer it was.

It couldn't have been long, he knew that.

In all his lifetimes in the past, he had died numbers of times. A few had been sudden, but most had felt like this.

Exactly like this.

He had no doubt he was dying.

He carefully tried to look down at his body, but all he could see was red-stained clothes and blood dripping far, far too quickly from him and into the passenger seat that was below him.

He was bleeding out and quickly.

He still couldn't feel his legs and he could see one bone in one arm sticking out like a third arm growing from his skin.

He had died in the past, so he knew this feeling.

But when he died this time, there was no reset button. He wouldn't end up back in the crystal cavern.

This was in 2017.

This was for real.

Damn it all to hell. What had he done?

He could feel himself fading.

"I am so sorry, Sherri," he said with what little bit of air he had left.

And as the darkness overwhelmed him, all he could see was her smile.

CHAPTER TWENTY-SEVEN

June 9th, 2017
Warm Springs Avenue, Boise, Idaho

THE OLD grandfather clock in the entrance ticked to seven p.m. and chimed, the sound echoing through the front rooms of the mansion.

Sherri once again went to the window to look out at Warm Springs Avenue and the traffic going past in both directions.

She had done that every five minutes for the last two hours, she was so excited.

And so worried.

Something didn't feel right, but she had no idea what it might be. More than likely her fear of seeing Carson again.

And her excitement.

It had been a very long, yet very short, eight months since she had kissed Carson goodbye in that mine and returned to Boise. It hadn't taken long to fly in some great contractors after turning off the ghost. She set to work on the mansion with an intensity she had never felt before.

The progress had been slow over the winter, because she knew every detail she wanted and sometimes things just took time. She was following Carson's original plans and making the place into something he would be proud of.

She had so loved the feeling of staying with him in the mansion in the past. Now she hoped they could both live here into the future.

And maybe build the mansion a few more times in the past as well.

She looked out the window one more time. She knew he drove a blue Jeep and there was no sign of that.

She couldn't shake the feeling that something was wrong.

She knew that for him, only a moment would have passed since their kiss. She needed to remember that. She was the one who was going to have changed, not him.

She couldn't let her fear get in the way.

Eight months of work and dreaming of him had to have changed her some.

She turned from the door and looked around at the place. Three times she had been written up in the newspapers and magazines for the ground-breaking work she was doing on an old historical mansion. She loved that, because she knew that Carson had seen one of the articles and been happy about it.

She had had a firm deadline and she wanted to meet it. She wanted Carson to walk back into his own home, fully restored and modern.

And she had hit that deadline.

The entire time she worked on the mansion, she had known where he lived just north of Boise in a modern apartment in the hills. And she had known he was working on his final doctorate and was teaching at the university. But she had managed to not get close to him, although she had seen him once from a distance.

She even knew when Bonnie and Duster and Dawn and Madison had offered him his first trip back in time and gone with him and how for months after that Carson had spent decades in the past, on every trip first building the mansion that she was remodeling.

In total, he had told her that he had lived almost eight hundred years. That made her feel very insecure, but she tried not to think about that. Bonnie and Duster had lived far longer and they were still her best friends.

Duster had warned her that she didn't dare approach Carson now, because they had to first meet in the past for this present to work out.

"Even though he has only aged a number of months here, he's lived hundreds of years in the past," Duster had told her. "That's the man you fell for, not some college professor."

So she had agreed to stay away from him. Instead she focused all her attention on the mansion remodel.

And on hitting the deadline.

Now, just last week, all the work had finally finished, all the furniture was in place, every detail was done and she had loved it, loved living here for the last month.

It had felt perfect.

And Carson had now returned to this time as the person she had met.

For the first time, they were going to be together in a dual time, in both their real times.

She was so nervous, she felt almost sick.

Like prom night or something.

And the nagging feeling that something was wrong just didn't leave her.

Somehow, she managed to stumble through the next number of hours, telling herself over and over it was going to take Carson some time to get off the mountain and then drive to Boise. He might have even stopped and changed at his apartment on the way here.

Finally, at nine, she decided that she needed to make a salad and cook herself a light dinner. The dinner she had planned for her and Carson could wait.

By ten in the evening, she was sitting on her front porch, the very first place she had talked to Carson over a hundred years earlier.

The air was warm, but cooling since the sun had set. The traffic on Warm Springs Avenue was light, muffled by the large trees sheltering her home.

With almost every car she expected Carson to pull into the driveway.

By eleven she knew the feeling that something was wrong had truth to it.

At midnight she called Bonnie and Duster.

When Bonnie picked up the phone, all Sherri said into the phone before breaking down into tears was, "He's not here."

CHAPTER TWENTY-EIGHT

June 10th, 2017
Above the ghost town of Silver City, Idaho

BONNIE AND DUSTER picked Sherri up two hours before dawn and headed for the airport through the almost empty streets of Boise.

Dawn and Madison had checked Carson's apartment to see if there was any sign he had been there, but he hadn't.

Sherri knew he wouldn't be. She knew that the only reason that he hadn't come to the mansion last night was that something horrible had gone wrong somewhere.

It was clear that Bonnie and Duster thought the same thing.

She had no idea if it was in the time travel or on the road or what. She had called all the hospitals between Boise and Silver City and no one had been admitted matching Carson's description.

And Duster had talked with the different county Sherriff's departments between Silver City and Boise and there had been no accidents reported with Carson involved.

Then Duster had had a friend with the State Police track Carson's cellphone. It was either turned off or destroyed.

Carson had just vanished.

At the airport, Duster had two helicopters ready and waiting. Neither were running, but both had two-person crews in their seats.

The plan was that Dawn and Madison were to search up the road while Bonnie and Duster and Sherri in the other helicopter would go to the mine to see if his Jeep was still there. If the Jeep was still there, they would all be let out down in the valley and hike up to the mine to see what was going on.

That was as far as the plan went.

Sherri had managed to force down a few pieces of toast while waiting for Bonnie and Duster to arrive, and she had a sports drink in her hand, but hadn't opened it. But that was it. Her stomach wouldn't allow anything more.

She had changed into jeans and a light t-shirt with a sports bra under it and running shoes. The morning air at the airport was still cool, too cool for only a t-shirt, but she was so numb at this point, she didn't care.

"We'll have enough light to start looking in about a half hour," Bonnie said to her, putting her arm through Sherri's. "We'll find out what happened."

Sherri nodded. After the cry last night, she hadn't let herself talk much or even think about the worst case in this. If she did, she would burst into tears and be of no use to anyone.

Dawn and Madison nodded to them and headed for the far helicopter. The pilots and co-pilots were doing pre-flight checks and seemed almost ready.

Sherri let Bonnie help her up into the other helicopter and put on a helmet with headphones so she could hear all the transmissions.

Beside her Bonnie did the same and then Duster climbed in and pulled the door closed, nodding to both of them and then telling the pilot they were ready.

The rumbling of the big helicopter was amazing, filling all her senses. And if this flight had been for any other reason, Sherri knew she would have been excited about this first helicopter flight. But for now, this was just a means to an end.

If she had Carson riding beside her on the way back, then she would let herself be excited.

Just under twenty minutes later, they were over the old ghost town of Silver City. The sunrise was just starting to pretend to color the morning sky in orange, and the valley below was dark like a coal pit.

"About halfway up the other side of the valley," Duster said to the pilots. "That's where he would have parked."

Sherri could see enough when they reached a few hundred feet above the side of the mountain that there was no Jeep parked there. She could barely see the old mine tailings and the shack.

"Circle around a few times in this area," Duster said, "in case he parked under a tree."

They circled for ten minutes, and with each passing minute the hillside became clearer as the sun started to color the sky even more.

There was no Jeep.

Carson had come back and left the mine.

Duster reported that to the other helicopter.

Duster then directed their pilots along the hillside where Carson would have driven and then along the road into the valley.

"We're starting slowly up the road from the highway," Madison said.

"We'll come at the top from this direction," Duster said.

The helicopter moved slowly, staying a safe distance above the trees, yet not too high as to make a search impossible.

They hovered over the bottom of the valley and then started up the road toward the summit of War Eagle Mountain.

Nothing.

No sign of his car. Nothing.

How could that be? Is it possible that they had done something in the past and Carson didn't actually exist anymore in this timeline? She didn't know enough about the math of it all to even make a guess at that. But Bonnie and Duster seemed to think he was here.

As they crested up out of the valley and into the light, Sherri could see the other helicopter working its way slowly up the valley below.

"There," Duster said, pointing down the steep hill to one side of the road.

Sherri's stomach twisted up into even more of a knot, if that was possible.

"Can you put us down close to here?" Duster asked the pilot.

"Big turnaround on the new road about a quarter mile down," the pilot said.

"Do it," Duster said. "Then get mountain search and rescue up here as fast as you can."

"Will do," the pilot said.

Sherri had no idea what Duster had seen, but he was convinced it was Carson's car. She wasn't sure if she should be excited or terrified.

Bonnie was sitting between them, just looking straight ahead, no expression on her face at all.

Sherri had known Bonnie for a very long time. That was not a good sign.

The helicopter put them down in a wide, flat area where the new mining road turned and the road into Silver City left, then after Bonnie and Duster and Sherri were clear, took off to allow the second helicopter to come in.

Bonnie and Duster took off up the road at a run with Sherri following. All three of them still had on their helmets.

It didn't take long to get to a place in the road where looking over the edge, everything below was clear, even in the predawn light.

It took her a moment to see what Duster had spotted, then she did.

About five hundred feet below them was the remains of a blue Jeep, smashed against a few pine trees that had stopped it from tumbling another five hundred feet farther down into valley.

It almost didn't look like a car anymore.

No one could have survived that.

Sherri knew that.

She took off her helmet and dropped to the dirt off the road.

Carson was dead.

How could that be possible?

He had died on his way to see her.

She could feel the tears coming as Bonnie sat down beside her and put her arm around her.

In the back of her mind she thought she heard Carson say simply, "I'm so sorry, Sherri."

She was the one that was sorry.

This was all her fault and she knew it.

PART FOUR
Yet Another Ghost

CHAPTER TWENTY-NINE

September 19, 2017
Boise, Idaho

One year had passed since Sherri and Bonnie and Dawn had sat in the Brooks Garden Restaurant, eating lunch, and Sherri had told them about the ghost in her mansion stopping construction.

Now she was back, sitting in the same booth, listening to the same sounds around them of the waiters laughing and dishes banging together as someone bussed a table.

The place smelled of fresh oregano and French bread and she felt as if she was sitting in a jungle with all the plants, high ceilings, and wood tables and chairs and wall dividers.

Just as she had felt a year before.

Only this time she felt empty. Not angry at a fake ghost as she had been the year before, but just empty.

One year ago, in this very restaurant, the events started that had led to Carson Edwards' death.

She couldn't believe it had been a full year.

On that cold mountain road that morning they found his Jeep, it had taken search and rescue almost three hours to arrive and rope down the steep slope to Carson's wreck. She just sat in the dirt back against the hillside, waiting. She knew he was dead, but the confirmation had still hit hard.

She barely remembered Bonnie and Dawn helping her down the road to the helicopter and then the quick flight back to Boise.

Sherri had stayed those first few nights with Dawn and Madison in a spare bedroom and could barely remember Carson's funeral at all, other than the fact that it was packed. A lot of people besides her couldn't believe he was gone.

A lot of people besides her were hurting, including his parents. He hadn't talked about them at all in the short time they had been together. Of course, at that point he had lived upwards of eight hundred

Now Available
from all your favorite booksellers in trade paper and electronic editions.

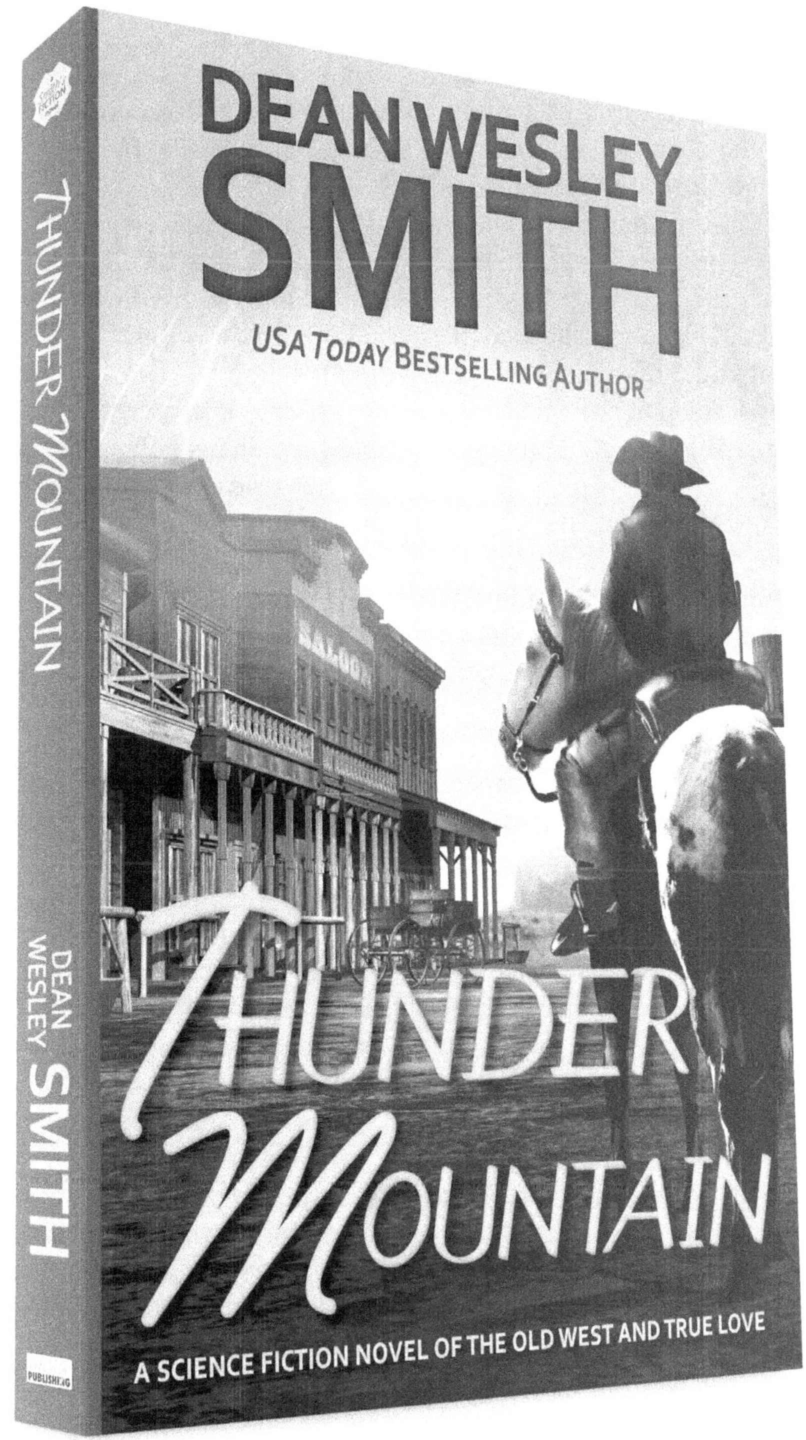

years without seeing them, so there had been no reason to bring up any family.

At the funeral in the huge chapel, she had sat a few rows back, staring at the closed coffin, holding Bonnie's hand. Outside, the day had turned gray, overcast, and cold. Just as her life had done.

The day after the funeral, she had gone home, back to the Edwards Mansion. A month before the accident, she had sold her condo in the North End of Boise, so the mansion was her home. And she intended to make it her home, just as Carson had made it his.

For the first few days, she had just wandered around the big place, thinking she was seeing Carson at most turns.

She had traded a fake ghost for a real one.

But after another week, she came to accept that he was gone. And she had stopped imagining he was there all the time.

She finally knew he would never live in the mansion with her as she had dreamed he would. And slowly, as the summer went past, she settled into what she called her zombie routine.

Her only chore, her only job every day was keeping up the mansion. She did most of the cleaning herself, most of the minor maintenance that needed to be done. She just wanted to be busy.

The mansion was still her focus.

Completely.

For some reason, she felt that if she moved on, she would lose Carson forever. And she wasn't ready to do that just yet.

Finally, on the anniversary of the day that she had told Bonnie and Dawn about her ghost in the mansion, she went back to the same restaurant with them where everything had started.

Bonnie and Dawn had been insistent and she just couldn't say no. She didn't have the energy.

She was dressed in her normal around-the-house jeans, a clean dress blouse, and her running shoes. She hadn't bothered with make-up or jewelry and had just pulled her hair back and tied it.

Bonnie and Dawn were both dressed in jeans and silk blouses. The summer was almost over, but it was still a very warm day outside.

They made small talk as the waiter came and went with their wine and salads. Then Dawn asked her how she was really doing.

"I only knew Carson for two months, but I live in his home," Sherri said, shaking her head and stabbing at her salad with her fork. "I think the loss of the dream, a possible future, is what hurts more than anything."

"So you fix the loss," Bonnie said.

Dawn nodded.

"Not ready to move on just yet," Sherri said. "I got rid of a fake ghost a year ago and replaced it with a real ghost. At the moment I'm fine with that."

"I didn't say move on," Bonnie said. "I said fix the loss."

Sherri glanced up at Bonnie, then at Dawn and shook her head. She knew exactly what they were thinking. She had considered it many, many nights while laying in that big bed in that big bedroom without Carson at her side.

"Thanks, but no. I have thought about asking you if I could go back and just meet Carson right after he built the mansion, marry him, live in the mansion until we both had to leave. But that would feel like ripping open a wound every time."

"You could do that over and over," Dawn said, "for hundreds and hundreds of years your time. More than any normal relationship here in this real world."

"I know," Sherri said, staring into her salad. And she did. In her basement she had put up white boards and worked over and over the idea of just spending twenty years, or even fifty or sixty years with Carson every time. She would eventually want more and she knew there could never be more. They would both be in a jail of the past.

It would be as if she was living with a ghost every time.

"Not interested, huh?" Bonnie asked. She seemed almost relieved.

"He would still be dead," Sherri said, tossing her fork down. "Every time I looked at him I would see his wrecked Jeep, his casket, and know it was my fault. He died because we met. So I'm very interested, but I just can't do that to him or me again."

Bonnie and Dawn both nodded. That clearly had been the reason for this lunch.

Then suddenly Sherri had an idea that sounded even crazier than she wanted to admit.

They ate in silence for a moment and she mulled over the idea until it didn't sound as silly in her mind.

She looked up at Bonnie and Dawn. "But I wouldn't mind doing that if he wasn't dead today."

Both Bonnie and Dawn had been looking down at their salads and their heads came up like they were puppets pulled by the same string.

Sherri wasn't sure why she hadn't thought of this before. In the two months she had been with Carson, he had explained as much as he could about time travel.

Most of the time the conversations, done over a meal or in bed after sex, had threatened to give her a headache. But what she did understand was that with every event, with every decision, there were timelines where an event happened and timelines where an event didn't happen.

She was simply in a timeline where Carson died in a car wreck. She understood clearly that there were timelines where he didn't die. Where he didn't go off that road. Where they were living together and making love at night and traveling into the past together.

"What exactly are you talking about?" Bonnie asked, looking puzzled.

"I want to switch timelines," Sherri said, smiling at her and Dawn.

Then she went back to eating her salad feeling better than she had felt in months while her two friends just sat there puzzled.

CHAPTER THIRTY

September 19, 2017
Boise, Idaho

SHERRI HADN'T said any more about her idea, but had asked if she could meet with Bonnie and Duster and Dawn and Madison after lunch.

Bonnie had agreed and called Duster. Dawn said that Madison was once again off at the same conference he had taught at last year at the same time, which is why he hadn't gone with them the first time.

Duster had said it sounded like a conversation that would need drinks and food supplied, so he had called the owner of the Brooks Garden Restaurant, the one Sherri and Bonnie and Dawn were having lunch in, and reserved a private room for one hour away.

The rest of lunch Sherri had felt almost bubbly in her excitement. Finally, they all had glasses of wine and were sitting around a large table in a private room full of far too many plants for a place that smelled of garlic.

Duster hadn't worn his oilcloth duster or cowboy hat, but he did have on dark jeans, a silk dress shirt with the sleeves rolled up, and cowboy boots.

"So what's this idea that has you all excited," Bonnie asked. "Since you didn't want to go back earlier and just live with Carson."

"You ought to have seen her change mood," Dawn said to Duster, smiling at Sherri. "Night and day."

"The idea is that I want to change timelines," Sherri said. "I want to live in a timeline where Carson did not die in that wreck."

"We all do," Dawn said.

Duster nodded, but said nothing. He was not looking happy.

"Why do you think you can change timelines?" Bonnie asked, starting to look worried.

"Because you all did," Sherri said, smiling.

"Not following," Duster said, putting down his wine glass.

"Carson told me the basics of time travel and timelines," Sherri said. "I'm not a mathematician or anything, but he did explain in layman's terms a few things you all have discovered."

Bonnie nodded and Duster just sat there frowning. Dawn just looked puzzled.

"Two words," Sherri said, smiling. "Monumental Lodge."

"Oh, shit," Duster said, leaning back.

Bonnie just sat there shaking her head.

Dawn laughed and clapped her hands together. "Damn if she isn't right," Dawn said. "We all grew up in a timeline without a Monumental Lodge. We jumped timelines to one that has a Monumental Lodge."

"That's not how it really worked," Bonnie said.

Dawn laughed again. "But that's how it felt."

"And Carson always had the Monumental Lodge in his life," Sherri said. "So he didn't completely understand what had happened, so he said you four just jumped to his timeline in some fashion or another. It was his way of explaining it to a layman like me."

Duster sat forward, his gaze intense. He turned directly to Bonnie. "Did we do anything critical in the last months since Carson died?"

"No," she said, shaking her head after thinking for a minute.

He turned to Dawn. "Did you and Madison do anything critical to the future in the last few months that you wouldn't have done if Carson hadn't died?"

Sherri watched as Dawn shook her head, clearly thinking. "Nothing at all I can think of."

Duster turned to Sherri. "Can you live with knowing Carson died in another timeline?"

"I can," Sherri said. "But if we fix this, will he be actually dead in any timeline?"

Duster sat back.

Bonnie looked shocked and lost in thought.

Finally Duster said, "Shit, shit, shit."

He stood and Bonnie stood with him. They both turned for the door.

Over his shoulder Duster said, "Someone pay for this room. We'll pick you all up at six in the morning in front of Sherri's place."

"Carson and Sherri's place," Sherri said.

Bonnie and Duster both left without comment.

CHAPTER THIRTY-ONE

September 19, 2017
Boise, Idaho

SHERRI HADN'T slept a wink. She had packed and then paced the mansion most of the evening, resting in her television chair for a while, then getting back up and moving. She was just far too excited to sleep.

She honestly had no idea what Bonnie and Duster were going to try. She didn't really understand exactly what had happened with the Monumental Lodge. All she knew was that they had all gone back into the past to build the Lodge, and when they got back, it had already existed.

Carson had explained that they had returned to a timeline where other Bonnie and Dusters had built the lodge. And because they had been touching the machine, they remembered both timelines.

But since Carson hadn't been there, hadn't been invited into the crystal cavern yet, the lodge had always been there in his memory.

In this timeline.

At 5:30 in the morning she took her backpack out to the front porch and paced there, letting the cool night air clear her mind. She had on jeans and a t-shirt and tennis shoes, and wore a Nike sweatshirt over the t-shirt. She had pulled her hair back off her face and tied it and let it be long down her back.

The traffic was light on Warm Springs Avenue, and about quarter to six Dawn pulled in driving some sort of hybrid. She parked in the driveway near the porch and got out.

Dawn came up to the porch and hugged Sherri without saying a word. Then the two of them went back to Dawn's car to get her pack.

Dawn was dressed almost exactly as Sherri, only her sweatshirt had a hood and was a Boise State sweatshirt.

"I couldn't sleep I'm so excited," Sherri said.

Dawn laughed. "I didn't get much either. Not at all like the last time we left this town this early one year ago today."

Sherri laughed. "If I remember right, I wanted to kill anyone who smiled."

"Doing better this time?"

"Much," Sherri said. In fact, she was so excited, she knew she was going to have trouble with the drive, not because of being tired, but because she was going to be like a kid wanting to get there now. And now would seem like a long ways off.

Time was always relative like that.

At that moment, Duster pulled the large white Cadillac SUV into the driveway and stopped. Sherri and Dawn grabbed their packs and headed along the driveway. Sherri had put in small ground lamps along the stone driveway and this early in the morning it felt strange to be walking on those stones.

Duster got out and opened the back so they could toss in their packs, then went to the driver's side.

Sherri and Dawn both got rid of their sweatshirts, stuffing them with their packs before going around to the large back seats and climbing in. Sherri climbed in behind Duster and Dawn behind Bonnie, just as they had been that first trip a year ago.

Only this time Bonnie wasn't holding pillows. All four of them were very much awake even though the sun was over an hour from coming up.

A moment later they were headed down Warm Springs Avenue toward town. No one said a word until they hit the freeway and Duster put the SUV into cruise control.

"So what exactly is the plan?" Dawn asked.

Duster turned on a faint cab light so they could all see each other. It wasn't bright enough to interfere with his driving. He also had the heat down, so the car had a slight chill to it, which Sherri appreciated.

"We spent the night going over the math," Bonnie said, turning in her seat some so she could talk. "We are going to try the best chance first."

Sherri suddenly felt her stomach clamp up. "What do you mean by best chance?"

"I went back on the first trip on May 24th, 1902," Duster said, "when we first met Carson. So from that point forward until we all leave together, the timeline is blocked to us. We can't be in the same place at the same time with ourselves."

Sherri understood that.

"So we're going to try to go back earlier in May and attach the cords to the same timeline crystal," Bonnie said.

"Then we meet and talk with Carson," Duster said, "give him all the information he needs to survive and how to hide that he knows anything, and then get out of there before May 24th."

"Problem is snow around the mine, isn't it?" Dawn asked.

Sherri glanced at Dawn. Snow blocking them in May hadn't occurred to her at all.

"Very much so," Duster said. "On May 24th when I went back last year, it was mostly clear. But I don't know how long before that. We're going to have to all go in together and walk out through the snow, down the valley until we can find some horses to buy."

Sherri wasn't sure she liked the sound of that, but to save Carson, at this point she would do anything.

"I'm confused a little," Dawn said. "I know that Madison and I have lived in hundreds of timelines over the year 1902."

"As have we," Bonnie said, nodding. "But in the timeline, or timelines, we went back to with Sherri, the one she met Carson, we had not."

"By our choice to go back to that point in time," Duster said, "alternate timelines were created without us in them. So if we are going to find one of those billions that were created where we all met Carson for the first time, we have to be careful to stay in the rules of those timelines."

"Otherwise we just get bumped to a new timeline," Bonnie said. "One without Carson."

Sherri just shook her head and watched the freeway flash past. It seemed like such a simple idea when she thought of it. But with time travel and alternate timelines, nothing was simple it seemed.

"If we can't get to him before we need to leave," Dawn asked. "Then what?"

"We back up to the previous fall and try again," Bonnie said. "But that's farther away from our first trip and has more problems with it."

"Like Carson believing any of this," Sherri said.

Bonnie only nodded.

"The math we did trying to figure out why that Monumental Lodge is sitting there says this will work," Duster said, "But I have no idea why we didn't think of it before Sherri came up with it."

"Being the dumb new kid on the block sometimes helps," Sherri said.

"I think it's called being in love," Bonnie said.

"That too," Sherri said.

CHAPTER THIRTY-TWO

May, 8, 1902
Outside of Boise, Idaho

CARSON HAPPENED to be walking up from his stable after brushing down his horse Sandy and giving her some food when he looked up to see four riders on horseback turn into his drive off the rutted Warm Springs Avenue.

The early May afternoon was a perfect spring day, not too hot, but with not real bite to the air. Wildflowers were blooming in various places around the grounds, giving everything a touch of rainbow colors. The oaks and cottonwood trees that towered over his mansion were all in full spring green and shading everything.

Below the bluff the Boise River was in full run-off, the sounds of the water over the rocks and logs like a faint music to the afternoon air.

He loved the spring in Boise. More so than any other season.

He stared at the four on horseback moving toward him. In many, many lifetimes of living here, and in the nineteen years in this timeline, no one had come to visit him since the construction crews had left.

In fact, no one in Boise even knew he lived here.

The four looked familiar and he started toward them, reaching the area of the drive even with his front porch before he recognized them.

Bonnie and Duster Kendal. Dawn Edwards rode behind Bonnie, and a stunningly-attractive woman with long black hair flowing down from a sun hat rode beside Dawn.

Duster had on his normal cowboy hat and oilskin duster, and the three women all wore riding clothes and sun hats.

He couldn't keep his eyes off the stunningly beautiful woman and the closer they got, the more he thought he knew her from somewhere. He just couldn't place where, but if she was with Bonnie and Duster and Dawn, that meant she was from the future.

His breath caught in his throat. He just kept staring at her. He had never had a reaction to a woman as strong as this before and he flat didn't know what to do.

And she was staring back at him, her dark eyes wide, as if she was staring at a ghost or something.

He stopped and they dismounted about ten feet from him.

Duster tied all four of the horses off to a tree while Bonnie and Dawn and the beautiful black-haired woman sort of stood there and stared at him like he was about to do tricks or something.

He had no idea how they had ended up in the same timeline as he was in. When he left, there had been no one in the cavern or the cave, and in two minutes and fifteen seconds this lifetime was going to last for him in real time, they would not have had the time to join him on the same connection.

So he had no idea how they got here or even why.

Duster walked back toward Carson, his hand out, a huge grin on his face.

Carson had never seen Duster smile like that.

"I can't begin to tell you how happy I am to see you," Duster said, shaking Carson's hand with more enthusiasm than he could have ever imagined Duster having.

Carson nodded. "Great seeing you as well. And Bonnie."

Carson nodded to Bonnie.

Bonnie stepped forward and hugged Carson so hard, it almost crushed his rib cage.

Dawn was right behind her with a hug, and he hadn't known Dawn that long. In fact, in the numbers of times that he had been with her and Madison, she had never done more than shake his hand.

As they stepped back, he could see tears in both their eyes.

He had no idea why. None.

Something was very wrong.

"This is Sherri Edwards," Duster said. "No relation to you at all."

Sherri had tears running down her face as well as she stood there, clearly too afraid to move, just staring at him.

Carson stepped toward the most beautiful woman he had ever seen and extended his hand. He had no idea what was going on, but there was no way he was just going to nod at this wonderful woman. Even if she was crying while looking at him.

She took his hand, and then without warning, pulled him into the most incredible kiss he had ever experienced.

He could feel her tears against his cheek and he flat didn't care.

He just kissed her back and never wanted to let her go.

He forgot everything but feeling this fantastic woman against him.

Finally Duster cleared his throat and said, "I think we need to go inside and explain why we are here."

Carson broke the kiss and stepped back, not letting go of Sherri Edward's hand.

"That is the most amazing greeting I have ever had," he said, smiling at her tear-stained face.

She smiled back, which made him want to just kiss her again.

"That was only a greeting, remember," she said.

Carson flat didn't know what to say and Dawn laughed. "You are making me hot just watching you two."

"More information than I need," Duster said, waving his hand at some invisible bug in the air and turning and heading for the porch.

And with that, all tension broke and all three women laughed.

Carson had no idea at all what was happening. But he had a hunch he was going to find out quickly.

Then, for the first time in all the years he had lived in this mansion, women walked through the front door.

CHAPTER THIRTY-THREE

May, 8, 1902
Outside of Boise, Idaho

SHERRI COULD not believe she had just kissed Carson. She had missed him so much, she couldn't believe he was again standing right there in front of her. She knew that the Carson standing in front of her didn't know her, hadn't had a two-month relationship with her, hadn't been in love with her.

Or hadn't yet, as the case was.

But she had been in love with him, been at his funeral, and lived in his home. She had missed him and at that moment she didn't care anymore. She had needed to kiss him.

And from what she could tell, he hadn't minded in the slightest, although he was clearly puzzled.

After they went inside, Bonnie asked if they could all borrow his bathrooms to freshen up and get out of the 1902 clothing for a time. Sherri was very glad she had asked that, since they had ridden fairly consistently from near the Snake River this morning, starting a little before sunrise. She felt coated in road dust and in a few places the riding clothes were starting to really scrape at her skin.

Carson had nodded to Bonnie, then glanced at Sherri. "Sure, let me show you where the bathrooms are at."

"Oh trust me," Sherri said, smiling to him. "I know where they are at. I am the one who remodeled this wonderful mansion in 2017."

The look of recognition crossed Carson's face. "I saw your picture and an article about you in the paper. That's where I had seen you before. Thank you for treasuring my home."

"Always," she said, following Bonnie and Dawn back out to the horses to get clothes. Duster than took the horses around to the back while Dawn and Bonnie headed for the main floor bathroom off the hallway.

"Mind if I use your master bath?" Sherri asked. "It's the one I'm the most used to living in."

He blushed and nodded. "Pardon the mess."

"Honestly," she said, "I will welcome the mess. You'll understand shortly."

After a moment, she found herself stripping out of her clothes and washing up in her own bathroom. The same blue tile, the same mirror, the same mahogany shelves. Only it wasn't yet her bathroom, but Carson's bathroom over a hundred years before. But she had matched so much in the remodeling that only the fixtures were different, and there wasn't a large walk-in shower cut into one wall.

So it felt like her bathroom. Only shifted slightly.

And having Carson's stuff scattered around the bathroom instead of her stuff just made her smile.

Then suddenly she began to cry again. She really, really needed to get hold of herself if she was going to save his life.

And her life and future in the process.

She spent an extra minute splashing cold water on her face, getting herself under control, and combing her hair and tying it back.

Twelve minutes after she had climbed the big staircase, she went back downstairs and into the kitchen, now dressed in her most comfortable jeans, a Stanford t-shirt, and tennis shoes.

Carson was there alone, fixing a tray of iced tea with real ice, just as he would do for her in August.

He turned and saw her and smiled, just staring at her.

"You look radiant," he finally said after a long moment.

She could feel herself blush. "Thank you. I can't begin to tell you how good you look."

He nodded to her t-shirt. "Stanford grad?"

"A couple of the degrees," she said, shrugging.

"I assume we have a history, or a future, or something," he said. "Or at least I hope we do."

"We do," she said, smiling at him. "I promise we'll tell you all about it shortly."

He nodded. "In the remodel, did you find the hidden room upstairs?"

"You showed me where it was at," she said, smiling. "Part of our future or history or whatever."

"Timelines and time travel can give a person a headache, can't it?" he asked, laughing.

"Without it, we would have never met, you wouldn't have built this wonderful mansion, and I wouldn't be here now either, so I like the headache."

He laughed. "Actually, so do I."

At that moment Duster came in from the back and took off his coat and hat and from down the hallway Bonnie and Dawn were laughing about something as they moved toward the kitchen.

"How about we set up on the back porch in the shade," Carson said. "The weather is perfect there."

Sherri loved that idea. She had spent many a late afternoon after Carson was killed on that porch. Sitting back there with him would erase some of those dark moments.

Especially on such a perfect spring day.

And especially with Carson at her side.

CHAPTER THIRTY-FOUR

May, 8, 1902
Outside of Boise, Idaho

CARSON COULD not believe how attracted he was to Sherri Edwards. In all his time, in all the marriages and relationships he had had over the last eight hundred years of living in the past, he had never felt like this for a woman.

It was as if he couldn't imagine her not being there, and yet he had only met her, and kissed her, just twenty minutes before.

But he didn't want to fight the feeling. It felt wonderful. And she had to be the most attractive woman he had ever seen. Ever.

And her kiss was something to desire again and again.

They all got settled on the back porch on chairs he had pulled outside from his kitchen table. They all sipped at their tea for a moment, then Carson decided to get the ball rolling. He could tell they were suddenly uncomfortable.

Carson turned to Duster. "Time for a story I would think."

Duster nodded. "This time we came back from September 20th, 2017, to about four days ago. It took us a couple of days to walk out of Silver City to find horses and get here."

Carson felt surprised as he glanced at Bonnie and Dawn and Sherri. A hike like that in soft, muddy ground or snow could not have been fun.

"Why did you come in so early?" Carson asked.

"Because on September 20th, 2016, we came back here to this timeline. I came in early on May 24th, so we have to be here and be back in the cave and gone by May 23rd to preserve that trip as best we can."

"You came here from 2016 later this summer? Carson asked. "But you didn't know me then. I hadn't been recruited."

Duster nodded. "Sherri was having trouble with your recorded ghost, so we decided to come back and meet the ghost before he killed himself."

Carson glanced at Sherri. "The batteries lasted that long?"

Sherri nodded and smiled at him, but there was worry in her eyes, so Carson turned his attention back to Duster.

"Bonnie and Dawn and Sherri came through in early August and we all met a few days later," Duster said. "You two fell in love and you decided to cut your trip short and head back."

"I came through to here on June 9th, 2017. That's over eight months later."

Duster nodded and all three women nodded, but no one was saying a word. Something had happened.

"Sherri fixed up the mansion and was waiting for you to arrive on June 9th, but you never showed up," Duster said.

Carson could feel his stomach twisting in to a knot. "What happened? What did I do?"

"You missed a curve coming over the top of War Eagle, on the old road out of the Silver City valley."

"I died in 2017?" Carson asked, his stomach completely twisted up.

Duster nodded. "It was an amazing funeral."

"Oh, shit," Carson said, standing and moving to the railing to look out at the river and the wildflowers. He wanted to just throw up. He had died a number of times on his thirty plus trips into the past because he had been researching World War One. It was a dangerous time. But after every death he always had ended up back in the crystal cavern just two minutes after he left.

He didn't like the pain of dying, but he didn't fear it anymore.

At least not in the past.

But Duster had just told him he had died in 2017. That meant this was his last trip back.

Sherri moved up and put her arm around his waist as if she had been doing that over and over for a long time.

"I know this is a lot to take," Sherri said. But you have time to understand it. Listen to why we are here. Listen to the experts in time and timelines."

Carson forced himself to take a deep breath of the wonderful afternoon air and nod. He looked down into her deep eyes and knew there had to be something.

And he knew this woman loved him.

He nodded and let Sherri turn him around and they both went back to their chairs.

"So I die going off a cliff on June 9th, 2017, trying to get back to this wonderful woman who has restored this wonderful home. That right?"

Duster nodded.

Carson turned to Sherri. "I am so sorry. I can't imagine what that put you through."

Tears instantly formed in her eyes and she nodded. Then she managed to say, "Listen to Duster."

Carson turned back to Duster, whose dark eyes were intense and very worried.

"You died on June 9th, 2017," Duster said. "On September 19th, Sherri reminded us of Monumental Lodge."

Carson suddenly felt very confused. He had never really understood the story of the big lodge up on the edge of the primitive area in Central Idaho. It had just always been there in his lifetime.

But Bonnie and Duster and Dawn and Madison said they had built it. But he knew and they knew that wasn't possible because when traveling, a traveler always went to a different timeline. Almost identical, but yet different.

Yet the lodge existed and those who had gone back remembered it always being there while remembering building it. He never understood that.

"Not sure how that follows or has anything to do with my death," Carson said.

"Sherri said she wanted to live in a different timeline," Duster said, "one where you were not killed."

Carson nodded, still not following.

"Bonnie and I grew up in a world where the Monumental Lodge did not exist and that part of Idaho was completely forgotten," Duster said. "We remember that timeline clearly. Yet we live in a timeline where the Monumental Lodge exists. And always existed. And since that is the case, we would have had no reason to go build it in the past."

"We want to live in a timeline where we have a memory of you dying," Sherri said, "but one in which you are very much alive."

Carson looked at the tear-filled eyes of Sherri, then back at Duster. "Is that possible?"

Both Duster and Bonnie nodded.

"The math says it is," Duster said. "But getting through the next four months until September 20th might be the most impossible four months you have ever lived if you are going to make this work."

"Why?" Carson asked, once again feeling panicked.

"Because you need to do everything, and I do mean everything," Bonnie said, "that you did before we came and warned you."

"If you don't," Duster said, "you will split off new timelines where you didn't die, but in our timeline you will still be dead."

"If you don't slip," Duster said, "then we believe all the timelines will merge back together into timelines where you did not die, but the four of us will have memories that you did. No one else will know, just as you don't know in our future timeline when the Monumental Lodge existed or didn't exist. To you it was just there as part of your life."

"No slip in four months," he said.

Duster nodded. "Nothing, not a one."

"We'll train you," Sherri said, tears falling down her face. "We'll make sure you save your own life."

CHAPTER THIRTY-FIVE

May, 18, 1902
Outside of Boise, Idaho

SHERRI STOOD with Carson, holding his hand in front of their mansion as Bonnie and Duster and Dawn brought their horses up. Duster had saddled her horse for her and was leading it.

The early morning was cool, almost cold, and Sherri had on a leather jacket over her tan riding clothes as a woman of this time would wear. The area in front of the mansion was beautiful, still almost dark under the canopy of tall trees. No one had passed on Warm Springs Avenue since she and Carson had come out here to say goodbye.

"I'm scared to death," Carson said, squeezing her hand.

"Even if you don't live in my timeline," Sherri said, "at least you will live in others."

Carson nodded. "I know."

"You can do this."

"I'm not so sure," he said. "But I'm going to try."

Sherri knew that. They had talked about it a lot, but now as she was leaving, she could tell that the next four months scared him to death.

"You got the script tucked away in a safe place, some place I won't even find?" Sherri asked.

"I do," he said, nodding. "And since you have never mentioned it, you clearly didn't find it in the remodel either."

She turned and looked at him, very surprised. She knew every inch of that mansion. Every inch. That notebook he had been working in taking detailed notes of everything any of them could remember about the coming next four months was not a small notebook.

He laughed, a laugh she had come to love, and would come to love in August.

"I'll show you after September 20th when you all get back," he said.

"And not a moment before," she said. "Promise me."

"I promise. My life depends on it."

"And so does mine," she said.

She reached up and kissed him. "Be nice to the future me, or the past me, as the case might be. Whatever."

He laughed again. "Was I nice the first time around?"

"Very," she said.

"Then I will be again."

She laughed.

Then she kissed him one more time, long and hard, and moved to her horse Duster was holding for her near the front porch. She didn't dare let herself linger. She had to trust the math of Bonnie and Duster.

She was either going back to a life without Carson, or a life with Carson. It would depend on how well he did.

Over the last ten days she had really, really wanted to sleep with Carson, but she knew she couldn't. She needed to leave that first time for the very first time in August, as it had happened.

She told him everything about their month-plus together, everything they did. But even though she asked, she didn't tell him things about herself. Bonnie and Duster had both warned her about that. He needed to discover them in the same way he did the first time, and if he knew too much about her now, he might slip.

And one slip would move the timeline over. He couldn't change a thing until he got to 2017. Then he needed to change the outcome on that one corner. And then live naturally with Sherri the rest of the summer.

And if he did change the outcome on that corner, he still didn't dare tell them about what had happened until they returned. If he could do that, then Duster believed the timelines would all merge and his death would exist in no timelines.

His death would exist only in four people's memories.

But if he slipped at all, billions of Sherris would return to a future with Carson still being dead. Sherri knew Carson was faced with an almost impossible task.

But she had a hunch if anyone could do it, he could.

"See you on September 20th, 2017," Carson said, waving to all of them as they turned their horses up the drive.

"Good luck," Duster said over his shoulder.

Bonnie and Dawn waved.

Sherri looked back at the man she loved standing on the huge front porch of their mansion. His mansion now, her mansion in 2017. And she so wanted it to be both of their homes at the same time.

She smiled and waved and then turned back before the tears started to flow.

Over the last ten days he had been so alive, so wonderful. If she returned to 2017 and he was still dead, she wasn't sure if she would survive the heartbreak of that.

He had to make it work.

He had to follow the script of his own future right to that corner on that mountain road.

And then he had to change that.

CHAPTER THIRTY-SIX

August 5, 1902
Idanha Hotel, Boise, Idaho

CARSON WAS SCARED flat out of his mind. He had told Sherri that he had enjoyed the ride into town just as the sun was cresting over the western mountains this first morning. The summer sky was a deep blue, with hints of reds shadowing high clouds. The air was still crisp and dry from the night, giving no hint of the warm day ahead.

He could understand why he would have enjoyed the ride, but now he just couldn't. Today it all really started. He had studied and studied the script he had, his actions the first time that Sherri had seen him. He needed to duplicate those actions exactly.

He just let Sandy, his mare, set her own pace and he focused on relaxing during the mile ride, watching the swallows swarm and dart along the river. Along the way he tipped his hat to neighbors and passing wagons. Boise in 1902 was a very, very civilized place.

And growing quickly. It was still only a small shadow of what it would be in 2017, but the bones of the larger city were now in place.

He loved the cool mornings and he actually enjoyed the hot days. In fact, he knew that every day until he left on September 20th would be hot. But since Boise was on the edge of the high desert and against mountains, the heat never held through the night.

He hadn't played much poker these last few months, just on the evenings that Duster had told him he had played. He had told Sherri that he needed supplies which was why he was going into town just at sunrise, when it was still cool.

He gave Sandy to the stable behind the Idanha Hotel and went in for breakfast. When on a supply run, he always treated himself to breakfast and for the last two years of his stay in Boise, it was always in the Idanha dining room. They served the best breakfasts in town for those who could afford them.

Sherri told him that was why he had come here this morning and that made sense to him completely.

He loved the big dining room with the tall windows and stone fireplace. It felt comfortable, yet had a formal atmosphere to it that he had come to enjoy.

This morning the hotel had the windows of the dining room slightly open letting in a cool breeze. Not enough to chill, but enough to make sure the room was as cool as it could be for the coming warm day.

Since the dining room had just opened at six, he was one of the first in and was seated at his normal table against the far wall, which was where Sherri said he had been seated. From there he could see everyone who came in as well as passersby on the wooden sidewalk outside the windows along Main Street.

He ordered his normal sliced ham, three eggs, and fried potatoes, taken a sip of his black coffee, and had his hand on the *Idaho Statesman* morning paper that he had picked up from the lobby when Sherri entered.

She wore a light-blue summer dress with a slightly plunging neckline and a blue sapphire necklace over smooth, perfect skin. She stood no more than five-four if that and was clearly in great condition. Everything about her shouted she was a woman of means.

He damn near started coughing, but managed to hold it. She was so beautiful and this was now very, very real and happening exactly as Sherri and Bonnie and Duster said it would.

Sherri carried a wide-brimmed light-blue hat in her hands and she had long black hair that was held up on the back of her head by an ivory comb. Her white skin seemed flushed, which told of either worry, or a few recent days in the sun.

His heart was beating and suddenly the cool morning didn't seem so cool.

He felt like he had been caught off guard even though he had prepared for this moment since early May when Sherri appeared at his home with Duster and Bonnie and Dawn.

He didn't much like that feeling of being off guard. He had to be on guard and relaxed if this was going to work.

He forced himself to take a deep breath and relax and just study her, since she had told him she didn't see him until after she sat down.

Sherri's dark eyes looked very worried and her gaze darted from one side of the room to the other, clearly expecting to see Bonnie and Duster and Dawn.

Her wonderful hands twisted at her hat and she seemed instantly uncomfortable, as if she might panic and flee out of the dining room.

Her cheeks flushed pinkish even more.

She stood there for a moment, clearly getting more and more worried as she kept glancing back at the doorway behind her and the staircase across the lobby.

A waiter approached her and said something that Carson couldn't hear and she nodded and said something in return.

Carson knew exactly what they had both said. It was in his notes.

The waiter led her to a table directly across the large dining room from Carson and held the chair for her to be seated so that she had her back to the wall and was facing him.

She thanked the waiter and he nodded and turned away.

Now was the time. He had to look cool and interested in her.

The exchange with the waiter did not seem to ease her tension. In fact, sitting there alone clearly bothered her even more. She didn't know where to look or what to do with her hands. Her gaze stayed focused on the table and then the hat still in her hands.

He unfolded his newspaper and watched her over the top of it so at least he didn't seem too obvious to the others in the room or the waiters.

Finally, he watched her take a deep breath and clearly calm down some.

A moment later the waiter brought her a glass of water with real ice in it and she thanked him with a smile that took Carson's breath away again. He had seen that smile for ten days back in May. Now it shocked him again.

Wow, she was the most beautiful woman he had ever seen. And that smile could melt a snowdrift in the middle of the winter.

This wasn't really happening.

"Calm," he repeated softly under his breath. "Stay calm."

He watched her take a sip of the water, then another deep breath.

She was clearly getting her nerves more and more under control.

He put the paper down as, for the first time, she started to actually focus on the people in the restaurant around her.

There were only four occupied tables total. An elderly couple sat against the back wall, and two businessmen sat at a table next to the front window.

She looked at both tables for a moment, then focused her gaze on him.

He kept staring back at her, smiling, as she froze.

Suddenly, she seemed very nervous again and her cheeks turned slightly pink once again.

He nodded to her and then looked down at his newspaper as the waiter brought his breakfast.

Thank god, he wasn't sure if he could have held that much longer.

When he looked back up, she was smiling and looking very relieved as Bonnie and Duster came in to join her.

He put the paper up in front of himself as they had said he did and pretended to read as he tried to eat.

A moment later Dawn came in and joined them.

He kept pretending to read, as they said he had done, and he kept pretending to eat as well. But reading and eating were not easy at this point.

He believed his life depended on him doing just that. Eating, reading, and staying on the script perfectly.

He knew this was going to be hard. He just had no idea how hard.

CHAPTER THIRTY-SEVEN

May 20, 1902
Above the mining town of Silver City, Idaho

IT HAD TAKEN them two full days to get to Silver City. None of them did much talking and the mood was somber. Sherri couldn't think of much to talk about, to be honest.

They had decided to stay in the Silver City Hotel that second night and walk up to the mine the next day. There was still a lot of snow between the mining town and the mine, so they were going to need to be careful and take the long way around.

She slept that night like a dead person, mostly because she was exhausted, both mentally and physically. And there was nothing at all they could do now to save Carson in their home timeline. It was up to him.

She knew he would return and not have a wreck in billions of other timelines. But in her timeline, she wanted him to do that as well.

She did not want to return to September 2017 and have him still be dead. But both Bonnie and Duster had said that was the likely outcome.

But at least she knew they had tried.

The next morning Duster took their horses and sold them to a ranch just below the town, then joined them for a silent breakfast.

At ten, as the sun was starting to warm the snow at the tops of the peaks around Silver City, they started off walking down the valley away from the town. There were very few people in the town at this point of the spring, but Bonnie and Duster didn't want to take any chances of them being followed up the hillside.

Sherri still had on her riding clothes, with a number of layers of clothes under them. She had also put layers of socks under her boots. She had on a sun hat and riding gloves, but the bite to the mountain air seemed to just cut through everything she wore.

The climb up the hill where Duster normally drove up seemed to take forever. They stopped and rested twice, and no one spoke at all.

They finally went across to the mine tailings and all four of them checked to see if anyone was looking before spending some time to clear their tracks from the snow, make some new tracks up the hill to an open ground area, and then finally open the rock and go inside.

Sherri just sort of stumbled down the mine following Bonnie with Dawn behind her. In the big supply cave, they all changed into their future clothes, then headed silently for the crystal cave.

In the big cavern covered in crystals, they all moved toward the wooden table and the machine. She knew in a few days she would appear here on her first trip back.

Now the trip to the future, her present, scared her more than anything she wanted to think about.

"Everyone ready?" Duster asked.

"No," Sherri said, but still moved to put her hand on the machine. She kept the image of Carson's face clearly in her mind, as if that would help him suddenly be alive on the other side.

But at this point it was all she could do as Duster reached to pull the wire.

CHAPTER THIRTY-EIGHT

June 9th, 2017
Old mine above the ghost town of Silver City, Idaho

CARSON LOOKED around at the crystal cavern after Sherri and Bonnie and Duster and Dawn vanished. His wires were still hooked up to the machine and the crystal.

Duster had been right about that happening.

Carson had followed the script he had been given exactly. Four long months of being scared out of his wits half the time.

And he had also enjoyed the month plus with Sherri more than he wanted to admit.

Now came the only real turning point. He had to make it off this mountain alive.

Then, if he managed that, he had to be very, very, very careful to not say anything until September 20th.

He put on a glove, touched the box with his bare hand, and unhooked one wire with his gloved hand. As normal, nothing seemed to change.

He carefully unhooked the other wire from the box, then the two wires from the crystal.

He took a deep breath. He was back in 2017. Sherri was waiting for him in his home, in her home, in what he hoped would be their home.

Carrying his heavy saddlebags filled with money and gold, he headed for the regular cavern. He quickly stored the money, then changed back into his 2017 clothes. It had been over twenty years since he had been here, yet only slightly more than two minutes had passed. That always felt very strange and this time was no different.

He headed down the mine, setting the alarms as he went as Duster had trained him to do. He almost missed one because all he could think about was Sherri and how wonderful that last kiss had felt just a few minutes before, yet over a hundred years in the past.

And how much he wanted her in his arms.

But now he was going to face his biggest fear. Could he make it to her alive?

He made sure there was no one outside the mine, then quickly opened the mine door and stepped out and let the big rock go closed behind him. The afternoon was warming up, but wasn't extremely hot yet. The air felt dry and the ghost town of Silver City far below looked like it had a few early-season visitors.

His blue Jeep sat across the narrow trail in the trees near where Duster and Bonnie always parked.

Climbing in behind the wheel felt very, very strange. No wonder he had crashed. That last trip where he had met Sherri had been his fourth trip back today. He had only spent an hour in the mine since arriving here today, but it had been a couple hundred years of living and memory since he had last driven a car.

Duster had always said it was like riding a bike, a person didn't forget. But they could sure be rusty at the skill and that's exactly how he felt.

And he must have forgotten it had been hundreds of years since he last drove. More than likely that added to the factors of the crash.

He sat for a moment, adjusting the air-conditioning and letting the car cool.

His hands were shaking on the wheel, so he got out and walked around in the warm air for a moment, forcing himself to calm down.

Finally, he carefully backed the Jeep up and then heading across the hillside on what seemed like nothing more than a goat track. He seemed to be moving about as fast as he could walk, but for the moment, that was fast enough.

He made it across the hill and down to the valley floor and the main one-lane tourist road into Silver City.

He eased up the road, going not more than ten miles per hour at top speed and staying almost against the hillside away from any cliff. Amazing how knowing he died going over a cliff on this road made him into the most frightened driver possible.

He hadn't even bothered to buckle his seat belt because if he started over any edge, or the road started to cave away, he was getting out of this car.

He didn't much like this narrow, twisting road along the tops of large cliff-like drops into the valleys below, but he had driven it a couple dozen times, so before today it hadn't scared him.

Now he could barely breathe.

The road was no more than one car width wide and covered in hard dirt and loose gravel. And the road was dusty and rutted from the winter run-off. In a few places there was still winter snow drifted in under the shadows of the trees.

As he managed to crawl his Jeep up and over the top of the summit, he could see the Treasure Valley and Boise out before him, wonderful and green compared to the brown of the mountains around him.

Sherri was there, in that valley, waiting for him. He just hoped he could get there.

He eased the car along the inside of the road going down, moving slowly, keeping the car in first gear as if driving on snow and ice.

Sweat was dripping off his face and his hands gripped the wheel like a vice.

Duster had told him which corner he had missed, so as Carson eased around the inside of the left-hand corner where he had died in another timeline, almost scraping the edge of the hill, he saw a doe and two fawns in the road.

He stopped and put the Jeep into park and just stared at them.

More than likely that was what had caused him to crash. He had more than likely tried to miss the deer.

He put the Jeep back into first gear and eased forward toward the family of deer, honking until they ran up the hill away from the road.

At five miles per hour, he managed to creep his way around the next few turns and finally make it to a wide area in the road where the old narrow road joined a brand new mining road that was two lanes wide and maintained.

There was a wide turn-out there.

He pulled the Jeep off to one side and stopped and shut it off.

Then he climbed out, staggered toward the ditch, and lost the breakfast he had eaten in 1902 with Sherri and Bonnie and Duster and Dawn at the Silver City Hotel.

Then he just sat on the edge of the hillside, staring out over the green Treasure Valley. He could see the buildings of Boise tucked against the far mountains.

They seemed so close and yet so far away.

Sherri was there, waiting for him. And if he had to walk it, he would make it this time. He had gotten past the death curve. Now he was no longer on script. Now this was a new timeline and he just couldn't mess it up before they got back in September.

He could do that.

But first he had to get off this damn hill.

CHAPTER THIRTY-NINE

September 20, 2017
Boise, Idaho

CARSON KNEW that Sherri and Bonnie and Duster and Dawn had all gone through to his timeline at 11:47 a.m. September 20th. So as Duster had told him to do, he had all four of them sitting on the mansion back porch at 11:30 a.m. waiting for a surprise.

He had served them all glasses of iced tea and Sherri had made some light cake slices for snacks, even though she also had no idea what the surprise was going to be.

He had not told a soul, not mentioned a thing for fear of breaking off a new timeline.

The day was going to be one of those perfect fall days in Boise, not too hot, not too cold, with no wind to speak of. And since there had been no frost in the valley yet, the oak and cottonwood trees that shaded the big mansion were still full green and lush.

The summer with Sherri had been wonderful.

That first night after surviving getting off the mountain alive, had been, by far, one of the best nights in his life. He had gone home, to the same house he lived in in 1902, yet modernized in just perfect ways.

And he had been greeted by a woman he had come to love more than even he wanted to admit to himself.

They had spent the full summer just enjoying themselves, working around the mansion, taking a long weekend to the Monumental Lodge, and spending time really getting to know each other. They had made no other trips into the past and were seldom apart.

He loved that.

But now came the day he had worried about. He didn't remember dying on that hillside back in June, but if the plan to merge all timelines worked, the four people sitting with him would suddenly remember.

He had no idea how they would return to the crystal cavern and then be here, but he trusted Duster on that.

He hadn't hinted at anything at all. He had followed script perfectly in 1902 and hadn't slipped even a hint this last summer. No matter what happened, he was going to be glad that stress of keeping that secret would be done.

Carson also hoped the wonderful summer of memories he and Sherri had just built would overshadow all the pain Sherri had gone through in the other timeline with his death.

He didn't want to be a ghost to her in any way.

Sherri was sitting beside him, Bonnie and Duster were across from him, and Dawn sat between Sherri and Bonnie with her back to the mansion.

Carson glanced at his watch. One minute.

"Please put down your glasses," Carson said. "Time for the surprise."

Everyone looked very puzzled, but did as he asked.

Carson reached over and took Sherri's hand.

"I love you," he said. "Just remember that."

"I love you as well," she said, looking a little puzzled.

"I know you do. You have proven it in so many ways."

CHAPTER FORTY

September 20, 2017
Boise, Idaho

WITH HER HAND firmly placed on the wooden box on the table in the crystal cavern, Sherri watched as Duster put on a glove and unhooked one wire.

She had no idea what she expected.

She hadn't asked.

She just hoped Carson would be alive. That's all she hoped.

So far, all her trips through time had seemed like nothing had happened when the wire was hooked up or unhooked.

But not this time.

As Duster pulled the wire from the machine, around the four of them a shimmering wave washed through the big cavern and the light from all the crystals seemed to beam even brighter for a moment.

And then the cavern vanished.

It was like the time she had been outside the mine on the tailings with Dawn and then found herself in the cavern. No sense of movement.

Nothing.

She now found herself sitting on the back porch of the mansion with Carson.

Duster and Bonnie and Dawn were also there.

The shimmering around her stopped and vanished like a heat wave off of hot pavement.

And then the memories of the last summer with Carson slammed into place, shoving aside the memories of the summer with him dead.

Sherri just blinked, staring at Carson.

Could the plan have really worked?

She knew he had made it home to the mansion in June, only an hour or so late. He had said nothing about why it had taken him extra time and she hadn't asked or cared.

And she remembered the wonderful summer they had spent together clearly.

Every detail.

And she also remembered the helicopter flight and his wrecked car and the trip back to try to save him.

Carson smiled at her.

"I'll be go to hell," Duster said, clapping his hands together. "It worked!"

That was all Sherri needed.

She sprang from the chair and into Carson's arms before he had time to move.

Luckily his chair did not go over backwards as she kissed and hugged him, crying like a baby.

"My turn!" Dawn said.

Sherri crawled off of Carson's lap and pulled him to his feet as a crying Dawn hugged him.

Then Bonnie did the same.

Then Duster shook his hand just as hard as he had done on the driveway in May of 1902.

"You did it," Sherri said to Carson. "I don't know how."

Carson just smiled a smile so large, Sherri couldn't believe it.

"You have memories of both timelines," Duster said to Sherri. "Can you remember any differences before the wreck?"

Sherri thought back, holding Carson's hand so hard she was afraid she might hurt him. But she couldn't stop, couldn't let go for fear he would not be there if she did.

"Nothing," she said, after a moment. "Nothing."

"Then more than likely all the timelines have merged," Duster said, smiling and again clapping his hands. "We are the only four that remember the crash that now never happened."

Once again she hugged and kissed Carson.

She had just spent a wonderful summer with him.

And she had just spent a horrible summer after his death.

The same summer.

Two different timelines, now merged into one where the wreck never happened.

She remembered both clearly. But now, here, Carson was alive. And that was all that mattered.

Now they could put a lot of years between this last summer and the present, make so many hundreds of years of memories together that the half memory she had of his death would no longer matter.

Only the summer of being with him mattered.

That was now her only true timeline.

She hugged him and kissed him again. She knew, without a doubt, she was going to be doing a lot of that.

CHAPTER FORTY-ONE

September 20, 1897
Outside of Boise, Idaho

SHERRI STOOD with Carson on the edge of the empty parcel of land he had just bought that would hold their home, the Edwards Mansion.

The day was cool, the afternoon air promising an early fall. The oak and cottonwood trees covering the property were still in full green. Brush filled the edge of the bluff that went down to the river beyond.

They had tied their horses up to some brush near the rutted wagon trail that would be called Warm Springs Avenue at some point fairly soon.

"Are you sure you want to do this?" Carson asked.

"Did you stand here like this every time before when you built the mansion?" Sherri asked, looking up at the man she loved.

"I did," he said, smiling at her. "And every time I decided to build the mansion again."

"So you build it again this time," she said.

"We build it again," he said.

"No, you build it and I'll watch," she said. "I don't want to do anything to change anything about our wonderful home."

He nodded. "I don't either, to be honest."

She could, in her mind's eye, see the big mansion sitting there, stately among the trees. It seemed like an impossible task standing here now with just open ground, but she knew Carson could do it and had done it thirty-one times before.

And he seemed to want to do it again.

Then they would fake his death in twenty years and head for Europe together. She really wanted to research some of the homes of the period in France for a rehabilitation project she had taken on and clients who like turn-of-the-century French décor.

But after the construction of their home was finished next spring, they would have a wonderful twenty years together in the mansion before heading to Europe.

That sounded perfect to her.

Then, after this trip back in time, maybe they would live a few more lifetimes here in the mansion together, building it again, living in it again, and then traveling together around the world.

She wanted to put a lot of years between a present time and the half memory of that summer.

Together, they stood, arm-in-arm, staring at the empty ground where their home would be.

And where in the future it now stood.

Available Now!

From all your favorite booksellers in trade paper and electronic editions.

#1... October 2013

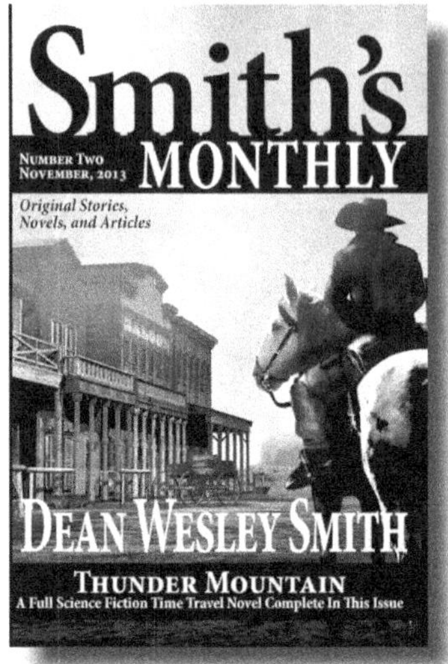

#2... November 2013

#3... December 2013

#4... January 2014

#5... February 2014

#6... March 2014

The First Full Year of Smith's Monthly!!!

Subscribe Now and start with any issue.
All are also available from all your favorite booksellers in trade paper and electronic editions.

www.smithsmonthly.com

#7... April 2014

#8... May 2014

#9... June 2014

#10... July 2014

#11... August 2014

#12...September 2014

Don't Miss an Issue!

Subscribe

Electronic Subscription:

6 Issues... $29.99

12 Issues... $49.99

Paper Subscription:

6 Issues... $59.99

12 Issues... $99.99

And Continuing into Year #2. Don't Miss an Issue!

Coming Next Issue in Smith's Monthly

A return to the Cold Poker Gang mysteries in a brand new novel

COLD CALL

www.ingramcontent.com/pod-product-compliance
Lightning Source LLC
Chambersburg PA
CBHW081152170626
46813CB00009B/3166

* 9 7 8 1 5 6 1 4 6 6 5 7 3 *